Thy Father's Glass

INDIGORIVER
PUBLISHING

Thy Father's Glass

JEFFRAY HARRISON

Thy Father's Glass

© 2023 by Jeffray Harrison

Editors: Adrienne Horn, Deborah Froese
Cover Design and Interior Design: Emma Elzinga

Indigo River Publishing
3 West Garden Street, Ste. 718
Pensacola, FL 32502
www.indigoriverpublishing.com

Ordering Information:
Quantity Sales: Special discounts are available on quantity purchases by corporations, associations, and others. For details, contact the publisher at the address above.

Orders by US trade bookstores and wholesalers: Please contact the publisher at the address above.

Library of Congress Control Number: 2022918133
ISBN: 978-1-954676-40-4 (paperback) 978-1-954676-41-1 (ebook)
First Edition

With Indigo River Publishing, you can always expect great books, strong voices, and meaningful messages. Most importantly, you'll always find . . . *words worth reading.*

For Ty, Miles, Nina, LaRue, Janelle, Selah, and Karter, in that order.

1

DANE SCHOTTMER SAT down front in the church his parents had attended for over forty years and stared at his mother's coffin. From his position, he could barely see his mother's serene half-smile or her gently closed eyes, yet it pained him to look anywhere else. Mid-morning sunlight streamed through the floor to ceiling stained-glass windows. It made Dane sweat under the collar of his suit jacket and cast a surreal flood of colors over the entire front of the church. A pang of guilt constricted his chest as he tried to remember the last time he had been in this church—or any church.

As much as he loved his mother, he hated being on display like this, hated the pity and concern of everyone who could never know the goodness and wonder of Gwen Schottmer's soul. The organist played one of his mother's favorite hymns, and a slideshow of her life scrolled by on the screen above the sanctuary platform.

He looked to his left where his wife sat. Muriel's dark, natural curls peeked out from a respectful black headwrap. His hand slid along the pew until it found hers and gripped it tightly. She looked at him through beautifully round black eyes, now wet and bloodshot. Her eyebrows arched slightly in an expression he had seen hundreds of times over fifteen years of marriage, asking *You okay?* He met her gaze and nodded, his toes clinging to the precipice. Her concern nearly pushed him over the edge. His teeth grit tightly together and his eyes burned fiercely. It took every bit of concentration he had to keep them from betraying him.

As a distraction, he broke eye contact with Muriel and looked past her to his father, Branson. The old man seemed completely oblivious to the entire situation, sitting up and mooning around like a toddler lost in the grocery store. Branson leaned over to his nurse, Sabine. He whispered in her ear like a child, loud enough for people nearby to hear. "When are we going home?"

When Sabine turned to reply, her brown cheeks glowed wet with tears. She calmly patted Branson's knee and turned towards the front of the church.

Everyone in the pew, including the pastor seated at the end, seemed intensely affected by the music and the speakers—everyone except his father. Seeing the old man's indifference caused a rush of anger through Dane's back and arms. He squeezed Muriel's hand tighter, and she squeezed back without looking at him.

The music had stopped. Dane didn't know for how long. That meant it was his turn to speak. He slid his hand out of Muriel's and walked slowly up the steps of the platform, drawing a folded paper from his coat pocket as he neared the pulpit. Flattening the paper in front of him, he looked over the people gathered for the funeral. A nervous pain shot through him. All those faces looking to him for wisdom and comfort, all waiting for him to say the thing that would make this all right.

Dane had labored over his speech for days, basically since the day his mother had died. He struggled for the right things to say to honor her, the right memories to share, memories that would color in the blank spots of her life for everyone who couldn't possibly know the fulness of her beauty and kindness and love as well as he did.

He had to come through for them.

He gazed down at his mother's body resting in the coffin. Her hands were folded, her hair styled neatly as if she were going to Sunday service, but she carried none of the warmth and beauty that had nourished and guided him all his life. Muriel had made sure the funeral home dressed Mom in her favorite dress, the black one that accentuated her height and, Mom would say, her long legs.

Dane gripped the edges of the podium and turned to look up at the portrait of his mother on the screen behind him. He remembered taking the photo on Mother's Day last year, remembered spending the day with her at the museum, just the two of them talking about each exhibit. He wanted to etch that picture into his memory like an old master's silver cast. But as much as the thought warmed him, neither his memory nor a flat digital photo could come close to the real woman.

She was gone.

Her warmth and life and beauty existed now only in his mind, and it might die with him someday or fade away, like so many memories seemed to have faded for Branson. Dane started reading his speech, refusing to show tears in front of his wife, in front of all these people, in front of his father.

When he told the story about his mother putting Christmas gift bags together for all her preschool students, he looked down at the front pew. Muriel locked onto his face as if she were trying to send wordless encouragement. Branson, on the other hand, sat up like a bored or confused child, looking around the room as if his wife didn't lie dead in front of him.

Words spilled out of Dane's mouth, stories and insights he had agonized over. Yesterday he had felt so proud of capturing his feelings about his mother. He had read his words to Muriel with theatrical flourishes practiced to perfection. Now they all felt like nonsense. He looked at the crowd, just as he had planned, and mentioned how she had touched all their lives in some way. He shared a story about her encouragement to play sports, audition for theater, and do anything he set his mind to. But none of these words held any power or meaning now that she was gone. Some of the beauty had left his life.

He felt like an orphan. In a way, it was true, because his mother had died, and his father gawked around aimlessly, not truly present either.

Dane reached the bottom of the page, and he realized the crescendo of emotion he had planned for the conclusion no longer mattered. Muriel cried in the front row, and at least half of his mother's congregation dabbed their eyes, wrapped up in his speech. He struggled for the calm likeness of unbroken, glassy water. Then he heard his voice break, felt his cheeks flush as if he had shoved his face into the hot oven. He looked away from the gathered mourners, away from his wife and her tears, away from everyone and everything that might set him off, and stared at the last couple of sentences in front of him. He mashed his fist into his eye socket to hold the emotion in, to grind it back where it came from. Then his gaze rested on Branson, still looking around and shifting from side to side, still oblivious.

A wave of old anger rose. His father had never been there for him, wasn't there for him now. Instead, the old man was embarrassing him and his mother all over again.

"Pop, cut it out," he barked and caught his father's surprised eyes. His father looked somehow confused and ashamed at the same time. They held each other's gaze. Dane's eyes grew hotter, and angry tears dripped onto his well-crafted speech. He mashed his fist into his eye to stop the tears. The people in front of him murmured to each other. Trying to speak again seemed overwhelming and futile. His voice had vanished, and he had made a fool of himself.

Knowing he had failed his duty to his mother, Dane descended the steps, shoving the unfinished speech into his pocket. He sat next to Muriel. She patted his thigh three times and then gripped it tightly. The pats said, *I love you. I know this is hard and I'm here for you*, and the grip said, *but you were wrong for calling out your father*.

Dane covered her hand with his and nodded without meeting her eyes. She slid her arm around him and kissed him on the cheek above the edge of his neatly trimmed beard.

For years, Dane had taught his students about catharsis and how moments like this were supposed to be cleansing, an emotional burst followed by the sweetest peace. But he didn't feel cleansed or peaceful. Instead, he felt angry at his mother for leaving him alone with his father, angry at his father for being so oblivious and unaffected, angry at everyone else for thinking they could possibly know what he had lost. But he squelched all that anger inside and went through the expected motions. He floated through the remaining rituals, only allowing himself to surface when Muriel or someone else asked a question.

Never had he been more grateful for Sabine and Muriel, who managed his father so well that he didn't have to look at the man again for the rest of the day.

If he asked, Muriel would tell him—basically had told him—that his outburst was his own fault, for letting his father's behavior get to him, for not understanding that this was the new normal, the best Branson could do. Dane refused to accept such a paltry offering for so many sins. Long before the funeral, before the senility and Alzheimer's, the decades vacillated between suffocating harshness and neglectful absence.

Dane recalled an endless parade of his father's failures, moments of importance to him when his father just hadn't shown up, or worse, moments when he had shown up and destroyed them with meanness. Nobody saw those failures now. They only saw the doddering old man, cute in his harmless inconvenience and awkwardness. Dane knew the strict father with harsh criticism, a ready belt, and not much else. This new man was a façade, a trick nature played on Dane to rob him of any chance for either reconciliation or retaliation. He hated it. It killed him to think the future would bring no apology or even acknowledgment for the past, and even yelling at the old man would offer no satisfaction. Only obligation awaited him now, carrying out the duties of a son to a father.

Sometime later, he stood at his mother's graveside, with all those in attendance ready to say the last prayers and let her go. Dane scanned the beautiful site, a green expanse of crosses and headstones with another reserved right next to it for Branson when his time came. Muriel held his hand on one side, and Branson's on the other, connecting them through her own life and love and energy. Later, they would all go home with their memories of his mother, and the next day he would sort out her life into boxes and somehow decide which parts of her to keep and which to throw away.

And, of course, deal with his father.

THE NEXT DAY, as Dane packed every memory of his mother away neatly in boxes, Branson sat on a crate by the attic window. The old man stared outside and occasionally laughed out loud at whatever he saw—or thought he saw.

The round, somewhat convex window in the attic gable looked over the yard more than thirty feet below and provided a fish-eye view of the neighbors next door and directly across the street. Growing up, Dane had thought the window made the house look like a cyclops from the yard, but he never told his father. Branson put so much sweat and money into fixing up the old family house that he would vacillate between sulking and shouting whenever Dane insulted it in any way, even accidentally.

But that was forty years ago. Today, at eighty-five, Branson just sat serenely in front of the circular window with the summer morning sun on his face.

Branson still cut an imposing figure, so tall his knees came almost up to his chest. His limbs retained their lean and muscular tone, even though his shoulders hunched and the skin sagged around his neck. His full head of stark white hair was cut into a fifties style with a part and a taper. Branson's blue eyes were grayer now, but his moony smile reminded Dane of the boyish grin he wore as a young man in the black-and-white photos Dane had filed away over the last couple of weeks.

Dane came across a box of old basketball and baseball trophies, some with "Branson Schottmer" engraved at the bottom, and some with Dane's name. Most of the little athletes on top had lost a limb or two, and "Most Improved" didn't have the same ring of triumph now that it did at ten years old. Years ago, when they were newly won, they signaled all the glory and pride of hard-fought victory. Now they were just pot metal, every one of them.

"Hey, Pop," Dane asked, "do you want any of these trophies?"

Branson continued staring out the window without flinching.

Dane stood up and held out one of the most intact of the trophies, a regional basketball championship Dan's high school team had won in his junior year. "Pop," he shouted, "do you want these?"

With his eyes fixed on whatever action was going on in the street below the window, Branson threw his hands in the air and let out a yell of excitement.

"Got it." Dane tossed the trophy back into the box. "I think you paid about as much attention the first time I showed it to you."

Tossing the trophy among the others and marking it for the garbage heap, Dane tackled the next box in the never-ending pile of junk clogging the attic. The label, written in his mother's careful print, read "Dane's Toys." Dane smiled as he opened the flaps.

The huge gray Voltron Castle of Lions playset struck his eye first, standing out in a kaleidoscopic mess of colorful plastic. He carefully pulled it out of the box, and a dozen or more plastic toys tumbled out with it.

Dane placed the castle on the floor in front of him, opened it carefully, and grinned like he had when his mother had first given it to him for Christmas. He ran his fingers over the lab and the launch pad, the cannons and the holo-table. When he first got it, he thought it looked exactly like the castle in the cartoon, but now he laughed at himself for ever believing it.

He had never had all the Voltron lions like a couple of the rich kids at school, so he could never play out his favorite scenes from the show. Still, what he lacked in funds he more than made up in imagination. The castle had been the setting for so many mixed-up scenes of heroism and childish melo-drama, so many crossover episodes for all his favorite shows and toys. Even though it was obviously just a big gray box with broken turrets and peeling stickers, it took a second for Dane to be sure he really wanted to throw it away.

He stirred up the remnants in the box and found broken Transformers and action figures, a blue Tron cycle with the action figure still inside, and dozens of Hot Wheels cars. Almost every toy had missing pieces or broken parts, but his mom had kept them all anyway. Dane laughed loudly enough to hear his own voice echo back from the rafters. He laughed at his moth-er's foolishness in hoarding all these old and broken toys, but even more at himself when he snapped out of the plastic daze, and realized at least forty minutes had gone by while he played with them.

Shaking his head, he filled the castle with smaller toys, mashed them back down into the box, and closed the flaps. He set it down next to the other boxes destined for the trash heap and brushed his hands on his pants legs. He turned to face the rest of the boxes, but then he stopped. Chuckling, he reopened the box and felt around inside. He drew out the Tron cycle, set it aside, and closed the box again. *The toy would look good on the bookcase in my classroom when school starts again, a conversation starter*, he told himself.

When he turned, he saw his father leaning halfway through the now-opened window.

"Hey," Dane yelled.

Branson ignored him, his shoulders now through the window frame.

"Hey, Pop!" Dane bolted across the attic floor and grabbed his father by his shirt collar. He snatched the old man back inside, more roughly than he meant to, and Branson's head clipped the top of the window frame.

After helping the old man sit back down on the crate, Dane slammed the window shut. As he twisted the lock closed, he looked into his father's eyes, wide and surprised as though he'd just been jolted from a deep sleep. Bran-son's brow twisted in confusion and fear.

The expression had become too common on a face that used to be so resolute.

Dane rested his hands on his father's shoulders and closed his eyes. He probed through Branson's thick hair for the wetness of blood or the bulge of a growing knot. He found a centimeter long laceration at the top of Branson's head. A trickle of blood began to matt the old man's hair.

"Stay here, Pop," Dane said, "and don't open the window again."

Branson nodded and continued staring at the front yard.

Dane jogged down the attic stairs and into the bathroom just to the left of the landing. He snatched the first-aid kit from the medicine chest behind the mirror and bounded back upstairs, two steps at a time.

His father sat stock-still in front of the window. Blood oozed down the back of his head toward the collar of his shirt. Dane grabbed another crate and sat next to his father. It took a couple of minutes of pressure to stop the bleeding, but Branson sat patiently, staring through the window. Satisfied that there was no serious injury, Dane leaned forward resting his left hand on his father's shoulder, his right stroking the back of his head.

Dane inhaled deeply and exhaled slowly, feeling the bone in his father's shoulder and the softness of his hair.

It was getting too difficult. In the last year, and so much faster in the month since his mother died, his father's focus and sharp wit seemed to abandon him. Had it really happened so fast? Had his mom just hidden the decline, or had he not cared enough to notice?

Mom had taken care of his father until she couldn't take care of herself. Then Sabine came to care for both of them, cook their meals, take them for doctor's visits and walks in the neighborhood, and get them to and from church.

So far, Dane's role in caring for his parents had been to pay the copays for Sabine's service and visit regularly to keep up with their health. More and more, he felt as if his efforts didn't count for much.

He opened his eyes and looked at his father's face. The shocked expression had faded and he was smiling again, staring through the window into the morning. What could be so interesting? Just a few boys, most around seven or eight, playing football in the street, nothing more. Dane hadn't thought there were that many kids in the neighborhood. Suddenly, a dull pain throbbed in his head, probably from the rush of adrenalin and the race up the stairs.

Dane checked his watch, grateful to find it was almost time for Sabine to arrive. She must have ideas about where to go from here. He took his father's hands and pulled him to his feet.

Even as a grown man, the eighty-five-year-old still had Dane by a couple of inches in height. Dane put his arm around Branson's shoulder and thought about all the things that never change and all the things that do.

"Let's get you some breakfast, Pop." Dane led Branson toward the stairs and stooped to pick up the Tron cycle as they went. "We need to talk to Sabine this morning."

By the time Dane got his father downstairs and into his favorite living room chair, Sabine was already walking up the front steps carrying two cloth bags of groceries in each hand. Dane patted his father's hand and then opened the door for her.

"*Mesi*, that's all of them," she said in a Haitian accent.

Dane carried the bags to the kitchen and set them on the little table in the corner where his parents used to eat. His mom's favorite pilgrim salt and pepper shakers smiled up at him, and he smiled back. Sabine opened the pantry and began putting away boxes and cans of food. Dane moved the bag of produce to the counter and opened the fridge.

"Make sure you wash everything before you put it away. Your father might not remember to wash those apples if he gets up in the night for a snack."

Dane nodded and took the bags to the sink. "How is Pop doing?"

Sabine put a box of pasta away neatly in the little pantry and closed the folding door. She shook her head. "It's like the ivy and the oak, you know?"

Dane grunted and folded down the grocery bags, stacking them on the counter.

"These old couples, they're so connected at the heart." Sabine took the electric kettle and filled it from the sink. "Once one passes . . ." She placed the kettle on the base and set it to boil.

"Just before you got here, he was watching the boys playing outside and tried to lean out the attic window. He bumped his head, but I patched it up."

Sabine nodded and took two tea bags from the cabinet above her. She looked back over her shoulder toward the front door and squinted. "I didn't see any boys."

"They were just out there throwing around a football. They must have scattered when you drove up." Dane sat at the table and ran his fingers through his hair. "The point is that Pop got so excited watching them that he opened the window. He was leaning halfway out before I got across the attic to close it."

"I'll check him over after he has breakfast." Sabine dropped the tea bags into the kettle, closed the top, and turned it off. "Mr. Branson is changing more than you might realize. He doesn't talk as much anymore."

Dane looked into the living room. The back of his father's head still rested against his chair.

"I cook spicy food for him because he says he can't taste anything." Sabine drew three mugs out of the cupboard. "But he still doesn't eat much."

"He's not eating?"

Sabine shook her head. "He calls me by your wife's name sometimes now."

Dane blushed and shook his head. "I'm so sorry. He's not like that."

Sabine smiled and dripped a little milk into two of the mugs before putting the carton back in the fridge. "I know. No worries." She looked at the pot of tea, growing darker every second. "They say, 'Once a man, twice a child.'"

"I wouldn't know."

Sabine shrugged, took up the kettle, held it over the trash, and dropped the tea bags in it. She poured each mug full and passed the one without milk to Dane.

"*Mesi*," Dane said, sipping the hot tea.

Sabine raised one of the mugs to her lips, tested the temperature, wrinkled her nose, and set it back down. She pulled three ice cubes from the freezer, dropped them into the mug, carried it into the living room, and set it beside Branson.

Branson looked up at her with a silent smile as she stroked his hair back from his face. Then she gently inspected the adhesive bandage Dane had used to cover the small cut on his father's head, and she pulled tiny bits of crusted blood from his white hair. When she turned back toward the kitchen, Dane quickly looked away, through the kitchen window.

Sabine washed her hands. She took the last mug of tea and sat across from Dane, in the same chairs where his parents had eaten dinner together for the almost thirty years that had passed since he moved out.

"You want my assessment?" Sabine asked.

Dane looked into his mug and shielded his eyes with his fingers. After steeling himself for bad news, he nodded.

"It's not long now. I've been in home care for almost fifteen years, and I've taken care of six families. This is just how it goes. Sometimes it's very slow, and sometimes it's fast. With your mother gone, it's happening fast."

Dane gritted his teeth and nodded again.

"Your father needs more help at night. He's not safe by himself anymore. Your mother couldn't do much to help him when she was here" —Sabine crossed herself— "but at least she could keep him from hurting himself or wandering around outside. He listened to her."

"Okay, fine," Dane said, rubbing the heel of his hand into his eye socket. "What do I do?"

Sabine carried her mug to the kitchen counter and set it down. "You can hire someone to be here at night. If the VA doesn't pay for it, you can pay for it yourself." She took the eggs, butter, and hot sauce from the fridge and placed them on the counter one at a time.

"Hot sauce?" Dane asked.

Chuckling, Sabine broke four eggs into a bowl and shook an ample amount of hot sauce over the yolks. "It's the only way he'll eat them."

"He always hated hot sauce. He used to act like ketchup was too spicy."

"Things change."

Dane drank the last of his tea, got up, and set the mug on the counter, trying to stay out of Sabine's way. "I can't afford to pay for care myself."

"Option two," she said as she beat the eggs, "you can stay with him your-self at night."

Dane thrust his hands in his pockets and leaned back against the fridge. He crooked his head and saw his father slowly drinking tea, staring at the dark TV screen. "I'd have to talk to Muriel."

Sabine nodded, moving the eggs around in a skillet.

"I'd need to leave at least half an hour earlier for work, and so would she."

Sabine lifted the skillet from the burner, flipped the mass of scrambled eggs with a spatula, and set it back down.

"I don't know if that's a long-term solution," Dane said.

"Maybe not," Sabine pushed the eggs around in the pan. She glanced at him. "How long do you think it's going to be?"

Dane clenched his fists in his pockets and tapped the back of his head against the fridge.

Sabine drew two plates from the cupboard, and divided the eggs between the plates. She placed a fork on one plate and held it out to Dane, smiling. She rubbed his arm and took the other plate to Branson.

Dane took his plate to the backyard and sank down to the concrete steps. He faced the patio and the abandoned basketball hoop where he had perfected his jump shot with hours of practice, hundreds of shots at a time.

Not once could he remember his father coming out to help him, coach him, encourage him. Instead, he only criticized him or barked orders at him. The only time he recalled his father attending one of his games was during his short stint as the coach of Dane's travel team, and after that one terrible season, never again. Not in junior high, not in high school, not in the state championship, not even in college when Dane had sent him tickets.

But now everyone expected him to drop everything to babysit his father?

Dane bit his lip. He couldn't tell if the tightness in his chest and the heat in his eyes were grief or anger or sadness. Whenever he had wanted to talk about his mother over the past two weeks, Muriel and even Sabine were there to listen, but his father was essentially gone—if he had ever been there for Dane in the first place.

And now Dane had to be there for him? To take care of him? It didn't seem fair. Dane still had to sort through the rest of his mother's belongings in the attic and seal every memory up, one by one, deciding what to keep from her eighty years of life and what to leave behind.

But what would he keep from his father? What would he throw away?

3

DANE HAD SORTED out all but five of the boxes in the attic, the ones he had set aside as soon as he had opened them. For different reasons, each one had caused him to turn away and focus on the kind of junk and clutter up there that didn't require much thought or emotional investment.

He pulled up a crate and sat in front of them now, breathed deeply, and grabbed the closest box, a regular white file box filled with a trove of greeting cards. It had kept the cards in nearly pristine condition although years of weight resting on top of it had crushed the lid.

Dane had always known his mother had been sentimental—the boxes of toys and school projects from thirty years ago spoke to her strong sense of nostalgia—but this struck him as something different and alive. Reading her loving messages in those cards was like hearing her voice float down the hall from another part of the house. When he first opened the box, a recent birthday card he and Muriel had sent his mother caught his eye. Muriel, always bringing a more personal touch, had written out her blessings and a Bible verse. Those words jolted him with their intense love, ambushed him with the thought of how much he had lost in his mother. Glancing over his shoulder at his father, he dropped the card back in the box and set it aside.

Steadying himself, he pulled a trash can over and took out a double hand-ful of cards. There were some from him and Muriel, some from just him or just Muriel, some from his father, from her sister, from people he didn't know. Birthdays, Valentines, Christmases, and all sorts of sympathy and thank-you cards.

Spreading them out on the floor in front of his feet, Dane touched each one, from the stiff older cards made from heavy paper to the slick newer ones with a slippery feel to them. He couldn't think of a legitimate reason to keep them, but he couldn't just throw them away. He had tossed out so many things today, and some things were trash his mother had hoarded, but others felt like losing a part of her with them.

If he kept these, they would go in a box in his own house somewhere and never see the light of day, probably until he died. But Mom had kept them. The array of cards on the floor included a Valentine from his father from just last year.

Dane picked his father's Valentine and caressed the red velvet front, the embossed gold heart in the middle – the most old-fashioned, no-frills val-entine possible. A typical corporate love poem decorated the inside with a curling script, but underneath the syrupy lines, his father had scrawled some-thing in his own austere handwriting. *Every year grows sweeter. Hope you like the chocolates.*

Dane couldn't picture Branson being romantic, and he guessed this scrib-ble represented the fullest extent of his charm. Still, Dane had to grudgingly admit that it was something. It took effort. The handwritten letters marched across the card's bottom edge like soldiers in cadence, but the feeling pene-trated the page, simple and direct. He hadn't heard his father share emotions much over the years, and now the old man could barely stay in the moment most of the time. But these couple of sentences represented the man at his absolute most emotional, and it was something. Take it or leave it.

There were other Valentines from his father to his mother, each of them about the same. Every one of them looked like it came from the bottom row of the store display, the cheapest and least ornate card in the bunch. Every one of them had a similar terse message handwritten by his father. *I love you more every day*. Another said, *You make life worth living*. The handwriting from one to the next told a story about the man's body and mind. Even if his mother hadn't stacked them neatly in chronological order, Dane still could have figured out which year each one came from by the slowly degrading penmanship. The earliest cards had the script one would expect from a small-time accountant and part-time basketball coach, careful, but not fastidious. But as the years went on, the writing looked as if it somehow got more careful and less legible with each card he wrote. The early ones were precise but with a spontaneous quality; the most recent ones looked like the scrawl of a child just learning to hold the pencil, with comically large loops and downward strokes digging ridges into the cardstock. Even the signatures started with the quick and stylized shorthand of a man who signed his name dozens of times a day for work and ended up barely legible scratches.

It occurred to Dane that these cards might be some kind of memory tool for his father, and maybe seeing them might help him focus on the present, or at least on some pleasant moment in the past. Before he knew it, he had sorted out the entire box of cards, throwing away almost everything, only keeping the ones connected to his father.

He had a handful of cards from the last decade stacked next to him when he came across a whole bunch of them from his mother to his father. She had given him cards for his birthdays, anniversaries, or other occasions over the years and then taken them back and stored them. Why?

It reminded Dane of all the notes and cards between himself and Muriel, the way his mother's cards to her husband had easily ten times the writing in them, so much more that the words crashed through the fold or spilled over to the backs of the cards. There were poems written in some of them, some verses Dane recognized, and some which must have been his mother's creation.

> *You are the rock I cling to when the waters flow over me,*
> *You are the star I look to when I need the heavens to guide me,*
> *You are the bridge that bears me over the chasm and sees me safely home,*
> *You are the heart of me, my protector and my pride.*

Throwing away those words felt like blasphemy. Maybe he was more like his mother than he wanted to admit. He stacked them in a separate pile from the others to keep, then continued stacking and tossing until he reached the bottom of the box.

Hearing slow steps coming up the stairs behind him, Dane got up and went to the attic door to see what his father might want.

"Can I sit up here for a while?" the old man said.

"Sure, Pop."

Branson beamed his son a childlike smile. Reaching up and patting Dane's cheek, the old man shuffled over to the window. Before he could sit down, Dane pulled his father's crate a little farther from the window, just close enough to see through. Branson eased down on top of it, hugging his long legs close to his chest.

"Now, Pop," Dane said, in the same loud and serious voice people use with children, "I'll be over here cleaning up. Don't open this window. You understand?"

Branson nodded without looking away from the window and put his hands in his lap. Dane patted the top of his father's head as he walked past him and back to the boxes. Branson laughed, mesmerized by whatever he saw through the window.

One down, four more to go.

One large box contained dozens of his mother's books. The bookshelves had already been cleared, and those books donated or trashed, but she had apparently hidden away the overflow. Since his mother had so many on display in the living room and on the bookshelves in the attic, he had forgotten about the ones he never saw.

Dane found hardbacks with worn weathered jackets and paperbacks with frayed brown edges. As he examined each one, he poured over his mother's notes scribbled in the margins and around the corners. Sometimes in the same book, different colors of ink held her thoughts and reactions to whatever she discovered in the books she shared with him, he even found his own name written in some of those empty spaces. *Dane's favorite part.*

He took out a leather-bound collection of Shakespeare's works, the dark brown cover worn light and thin in places. His mother may not have been a great poet, but she had a love for reading. She practically indoctrinated Dane with her passion for the classics. His infatuation with stories, his vivid imagination—even his career—he owed all to her.

Branson had laughed at the idea of Dane pursuing an English degree, not just once, but twice when he continued to grad school. Only Dane's mother had supported him, hungrily auditing the classes he took. She studied alongside him, often begging for the syllabus before the semester started and vicariously consuming every reading the professors assigned to Dane.

Carefully, Dane opened the volume of Shakespeare, turning pages that felt soft as silk to his fingertips. The pages parted, falling like autumn leaves to reveal one of the Bard's early sonnets.

Look in the glass and tell the face thou viewest.

Even before Dane had reached middle school, his mother read lines like that to him, explaining each one the best she knew how. His finger drifted down the page.

Thou art thy mother's glass.

Dane chuckled. He couldn't claim all his mother's wonderful qualities, but when it came to his passion for these lines, these images, these exquisite collections of words, he really felt like her mirror.

A sudden outburst from Branson snapped Dane out of his reverie. Looking over his shoulder, he saw his father rocking back and forth, clapping at something he saw through the window. The smile drained from Dane's face. What if he turned out to be his father's glass as well? What if he lost his passion for beautiful words, even lost the ability to understand any of the books he loved? What if he ended up like Branson, staring out into the distance and laughing at nothing?

A shiver ran up Dane's spine, and he dropped the worn leather book into the box. Then he moved the box over to the pile to be trashed.

The next box weighed more than any of the others, and Dane remembered it had his mother's jewelry box in it, on top of some other things. She had never worn much when she was alive for as long as Dane could remember, but she always liked nice pieces, especially ones with color and especially bright blue.

She would say blue made her eyes pop like a movie star. Branson would get her one or two tasteful pieces each year, and she cherished them. But then, as the arthritis in her hands worsened, she stopped wearing rings because they only hurt to put on and take off. Then she stopped wearing her necklaces and bracelets when she couldn't get the clasps open on her own.

Finally, even the pins and brooches became too difficult for her brittle fingers, and the whole box ended up forgotten up here in the attic. She had stored everything in there so neatly; necklaces and bracelets hung from little pegs, organized by metal and color, rings and pins pressed into little felt crevices and sorted by size.

The last ring was the most elegant—his mother's wedding ring. It was a delicately thin gold band with a beautiful but small cluster of diamonds and sapphires in a curled setting almost like crashing waves, the kind of lavish design his mother loved. It needed cleaning badly, but out of everything in the attic, besides the Tron cycle, it was the only thing Dane thought about taking home and keeping.

Turning it over in his fingers, he slid it up to the first knuckle of his ring finger, and it felt almost like holding his mother's hand again. He hadn't cried since the funeral two weeks ago. He had been able to push back every cloud threatening to break, but now the weather in him turned quickly. He glanced over his shoulder, a reflex from a lifetime of his father telling him to stop crying, but Branson just stared out the window transfixed, with a wistful smile as if he were watching old cowboy movies.

It took a couple of minutes to choke it down and be sure he could control his own voice again. He called out to his father across the attic. "Hey, Pop," he said, but Branson just kept peering through the window at whatever he saw down there.

"Pop," Dane said, holding out the ring for his father to see, "is it okay if I take Mom's wedding ring?"

Without looking at him, Branson waved him off. "It's okay. I'm just playing football with my friends."

Dane stood there for what felt like a few minutes, trying to make sense of it, trying to retrace how his father had gotten to his point. He looked at the two stacks of cards on the floor and snatched them up, ready to throw them into the garbage with the rest of the forgotten things. What would it matter if he did?

Instead, he took a breath, then another. Taking the tape gun from the top of one of the boxes, he tore off a piece a couple of inches long. He taped his mother's wedding ring to the inside of one of his father's terse Valentines and slid it into his back pocket.

How that man ever got a woman like his mother to marry him was a mystery, Dane thought. He walked over to Branson and put the stack of cards into his lap.

"I'm going to finish the rest of these boxes, Pop. Can you look through these cards and see if you want to keep any?"

"Okay."

"I'll be right over here. Don't open the window."

"Okay."

Branson set the cards on the floor next to him without even glancing at them and inched a bit closer to the window.

I don't know how to help him. I don't know what to do for him. I don't know what I can give him now, Dane thought. Something eluded him, a way he should feel about this, but when it came to his father, his emotions were like a well that had gone dry years ago, leaving nothing but dust and rubble at the bottom. Even the anger and resentment he felt towards the old man, as powerful as they used to be, were difficult to muster in the face of his father's weakness and deterioration. Even before illness took her, he had grieved so much for his mother, but now he couldn't summon much more than pity for his father. It reminded Dane of how he felt towards the end of a grueling basketball game or a punishing race, the feeling of reaching inside for strength or will to finish the course and finding nothing left but exhaustion.

His mother had invested in him in ways that his father just never had. Almost every book in the boxes behind him was one his mother had bought for him or read with him. He remembered trips to the bookstore downtown, his mother giving him a crisp bill and telling him to pick something interesting. She had read to him every night, well past the age where he could fit into her lap and only stopped when he got old enough to start playing sports for the middle school, when his fear of the boys finding out started to outweigh the delight he took in sitting on the couch with her arm around him, a book open between them.

In the last years, when her eyes started to go, at least part of his visits would involve reading the news to her or a couple of pages in one of her mystery novels. She would claim she had lost her reading glasses, but she always seemed to find them when she wanted to cook. He never called her out for it, afraid to break the spell.

Dane tried, but he couldn't come up with any memories half as pleasant involving his father. Over the last few months, he had forced himself to hold back waves of feelings for his mother threatening to overcome him at any time. But for his father, he had to force himself to feel anything at all.

He unpacked the rest of the boxes in silence punctuated randomly by his father's laughter as he sat by the window. He threw away almost everything else, barely glancing into the boxes, just to be done with it. To keep from barking at his father to shut up every time he erupted in laughter, Dane kept reaching into his back pocket and touching the ring.

After another hour, he finished the job. The room used to be his mother's refuge, but he had now completely stripped it of her presence. Her armchair and the small table where she would set her tea, all her books, the classical music she would play up there, whispery strains from the record player wafting downstairs and haunting the entire house—all gone.

The last remnants of his mother's things were the two huge bookcases, solid wood and wide enough to hold her expansive library. They stood together by the door, too dear to throw out on the pile in front of the house, too heavy to move downstairs by himself. Along with a couple of crates, they would have to stay until Dane thought of something better to do with them. He took Branson by the arm and led him downstairs, closing the attic door behind him.

4

DANE HAD ALREADY made three orderly piles of clothes on the bed and had started to pack when Muriel got home from the gym. He told her what Sabine had said and that his father needed him to stay over for a while.

"It happened that way with my grandfather." Muriel helped Dane pack an overnight bag. "I was almost ten, and that was back in Haiti, but I remember it was just like this."

Dane went to the bathroom and scooped his toiletries into a blue drawstring bag with some faded company logo on it.

"I remember being very sad about it. He lived with us," she continued. "A lot of people had their grandparents with them back then. It was like he was . . ." She sat down on the bed, rolled a pair of jeans into a tight tube, and shoved them into the bottom of Dane's backpack, "Like he was disappearing in front of you, a little at a time, until he was gone."

Dane cinched the bag with his deodorant and shaving tools in it and sat down next to Muriel, his shoulder up against hers. She stopped folding his T-shirt and rubbed the back of his hand.

"He's a completely different man," Dane said. "I don't know how this happened so fast."

"The doctors did say it was coming. We were all so focused on Mom for so long, I guess..."

"But I can't even say I really knew him before. Now what?" Dane took the shirt from Muriel's lap and started rolling it tightly. She took another from the pile on the bed behind her and folded it into fourths.

"You know, my dad and my grandfather never got along," Muriel said, smoothing out the folded shirt and handing it to Dane. "Papa only ever had bad things to say about his father—he was stingy, he was rough—but I don't remember any of that. People change when they get this way—a lot. I know other families who went through it, and it seems like there are always two ways people change: they either get really mean and difficult, or they get really sweet and gentle.

"My father knew his father all his life as a hard man, strict to the point of being mean. But all I remember of him was him sitting with me on the couch, all hugs and kisses, being so grateful for anything I did for him. He didn't always know who I was, but I knew he loved me." She pushed socks into the front pouch of the backpack until she could barely zip it closed.

"Once a man, twice a child?" Dane smirked.

Muriel whipped him with a pair of his own underwear. "Did Sabine tell you that?"

Dane nodded. "Pop was like that too," he said, rubbing his eyes with the backs of his hands. "Then he wasn't much of anything. He worked a lot, I guess, and when he wasn't working, he wasn't interested in much of anything I did. You've never really met the man."

Muriel nodded, put her arms around her husband, and stroked the back of his neck. "You can choose what to keep from your father. You can look at this time you have together as a window of opportunity to create some memories with him that will be full of love and kindness, and you can replace whatever bad memories you have with these good ones."

Dane turned his head and kissed her, wishing she could come with him, wondering how he would sleep in the old house, in his old room, without her. Even worse, no matter how hopeful Muriel tried to make it sound, he dreaded the prospect of so much time cooped up with his father. He tried to create a picture in his head of what it would look like to spend that much time with the old man, and nothing but torture came to mind.

Conversation between them had always been strained and awkward, and now the Alzheimer's made it nearly impossible. What would they do? Just sit around and stare out the window together? Listen to fifties music on the radio and tap their feet in time? Binge-watch *Gunsmoke* until they fell asleep? A dispassionate sense of duty compelled him to go through the motions, but he felt no real desire to do it.

Dane and Muriel had never had kids, never wanted to, but he imagined it would feel a lot like this. Before Sabine had left for the day, she had cooked enough rice and beans and stewed chicken for them all, plus enough for later if the men got hungry. She had also walked Dane around the house and shown him her protocols for getting Branson ready for the night.

He wasn't so badly off that he couldn't bathe himself, thank goodness, but if nobody reminded him, he would go days without taking a shower. Make sure to lock all the doors around the house and hide things you don't want him to get into.

Fortunately, Branson was a tall man who couldn't bother to bend over for anything, so putting dangerous items on lower shelves and the backs of floor-level cabinets kept them out of his reach. Make sure he had everything he might need—water, light, books, remote controls—by his bed in plain sight. Think of his mental acuity like a power grid, Sabine said. Too much stimulus, too many stressors, and the whole thing would overload and short out for a while.

"He needs his picture of Miss Gwen by his bed, his bottle of water on the nightstand," she said. "You don't want him waking up in the night and wandering around the house looking for something."

"Check," Dane said, "Everything in its place."

Sabine nodded. She stepped closer and looked up into Dane's face, touching his arm to command his attention. "It's more than that," she said, dropping the pitch of her voice. "The way his disease is progressing so rapidly, there's a chance he could wake up and not know where, or even when he is. Try to look at it from his point of view, how terrifying that could be."

Dane's shoulders drooped and he searched Sabine's face. "You think that could happen?"

Sabine patted his arm and dropped her hand, still holding Dane's gaze. "It's going to happen, Dane. The plan is to minimize his stress and confusion in any way possible, keep his grid functioning."

The sheer urgency of Sabine's instructions overwhelmed Dane, but she tried to bring him back into focus. It didn't seem as if he woke up much in the night. He usually settled down for bed when she left at six and got up to sit in his chair, sometimes still in his pajamas, by the time she arrived at nine in the morning. He would sometimes take a short nap in the day, but Sabine said she kept him up and active as much as possible during the day to make sure he slept through the night since he was on his own.

"You make it sound like we're prepping a house for a toddler," Dane chuckled awkwardly.

Sabine agreed. "Once a man, twice a child," she said, solemnly.

Once he walked through Sabine's instructions meticulously, and left Branson safely in bed sleeping, soundly, judging by the loud raspy noise coming through the door, Dane felt unsure what to do with himself. It was the same house he had grown up in, his old room, the kitchen he had plundered for the first eighteen years of his life. But now it felt foreign, as if he were some interloper, some shadow creeping up the stairs and stalking the quiet rooms.

He checked and rechecked the door locks, cracked the door to his father's bedroom, and peeked through the sliver of space to make sure he was sleeping, which he always was, every time. The loud snoring actually reassured him, and he didn't know what he would do if the droning sound stopped.

He didn't dare turn on the television for fear of waking up or, even worse, alarming his father, but he had brought some books. After deciding to sleep on the couch instead of his old room, he remembered to check the attic window to maintain readiness.

Dane had a vision that made him shiver as he crept upstairs to the attic. He saw his father laughing and leaning out of the open window, with nobody there to stop him or pull him back in. Checking and rechecking the lock put him more at ease, but he wanted more security than the little turning sash lock could provide.

There wasn't much left up there since he had cleared it out—the empty bookcases, a few crates, a broom and dustpan, and some folding chairs—but he placed every object strategically to get in an old man's way if he should try to get to the window.

Brooms would crash to the floor if the door opened, crates would topple over and clatter, and metal chairs would have to be relocated just to get in front of the window. As he stood surveying his work, he felt a little pride over what he had done, enough confidence to help him fall asleep tonight.

Still, he needed to check the window lock again. The feeling of having forgotten something or of having left the stove on after going to work compelled him to take one last look and reassure himself that he could rest for the night. He tiptoed around the crates and chairs so he wouldn't have to reset the trap and turned the lock as far as it would go.

The window gave a wide, pleasant view of the neighborhood. He could see why his father liked sitting there, even if he did seem to lose himself in a weird way. He got his face as close to the glass as he could and tried to see how far he could look down both sides of the sleepy suburban street. A sort of dizzy feeling came over him as he leaned into the window, as if the height of his vantage point or the memory of his father's near accident disturbed his sense of ease. Blinking his eyes rapidly to shake off the queasy feeling, he settled back on his heels and looked through the window again.

Neatly mown and manicured lawns all the way down to each corner showed how much pride and love the neighbors had for their homes. Some houses still had lights on, mostly upstairs, but a lot had gone completely dark already.

Many of the houses had the same layout, in three or four different variations, and some were exactly like the Shottmers', although none of them had the round window like the one he looked through. Not much had changed since he had played in those yards and taken the bus to school from that corner.

One thing seemed out of place. Someone had parked an old black car in front of the Shottmers' house. Not just old, but classic, like the cars in black-

and-white movies from the forties and fifties. To Dane, it looked like a specific one he remembered from somewhere, a Buick, or maybe a Pontiac, but he didn't really know much about modern cars, much less ones from over a half-century ago.

Still, it was one of the most beautiful cars he had seen. The rounded hood looked like a bullet or a torpedo, the smooth curve from the back to the front, ending in the raised headlights like eyes on either side. And whoever owned kept it so well maintained, it looked brand-new. The black paint glowed underneath the streetlight. He could barely spare a thought to wonder why someone would park on his side of the street or whose car it could be when he saw something else that made him feel dizzy all over again.

His father was walking across the lawn toward the car.

"No," Dane muttered under his breath. "Dammit, no, no, no."

He tried not to yell or make a ruckus that might startle his father, but he skipped every other step as he ran downstairs. The vision of his father wandering the streets at night plagued him until he burst through the front door and leaped off the porch onto the lawn. Once his feet touched the grass, he stopped so suddenly he almost flopped forward. He stood there in the creeping darkness of late evening and looked around.

There was nobody there—no car parked on the street, no father in the yard.

He turned to the left and saw his own car parked at the end of the driveway, all the way over to the side to leave room for Sabine to park in the morning. He turned toward the house and then back to the street again, confused and alarmed.

Could someone have taken his father? A car that old would have made some noise for sure, but maybe he missed it in his panic. Was his father's door open as he ran downstairs? He dashed back into the house and closed the front door, more quietly than he had run out of it, half sensing what he would find on the second floor.

His father's bedroom door was closed. For at least the fifth time tonight, Dane opened it just enough to peek through, but he didn't even have to look to know his father was still in there and still sleeping. The unbroken drone of his snoring confirmed it.

Dane wobbled a little, as if he had stood up too fast, and felt his way back to the attic stairway behind him, eyes still on the cracked doorway with his father sleeping on the other side. He carefully dropped onto the second step, his breath coming heavy now, and tried to slow his heart rate the way he had learned to do during an important basketball game.

Once he felt steady, he closed the bedroom door and crept back up to the attic. Everything just as he'd left it. He again maneuvered around his traps and looked through the window. The black car was back, and his father leaned into the passenger's seat, rummaging through the glove box.

He closed his eyes for a moment or two and then looked again, but nothing had changed. True, the darkness of the late evening made it difficult to see the yard, but there was no mistaking his father's stature framed in the light from the car's interior—his sharp shoulders, long neck, and his gray hair cropped close. He opened the window as quietly as he could, as if, for some reason, he thought the car and the man might disappear.

They didn't. Through the open window, he could see them even more clearly. He thought about calling down there, but he couldn't wrap his head around the situation enough to worry whether he would be startling his father, waking him up, or shouting at someone else entirely.

After a few more moments of staring, he closed and locked the window, and as he backed away, tripping over one of the crates he had set for his father, he could still see the old black car, still see the man now sitting in the passenger's seat rifling through some papers.

He couldn't feel his feet touch the floor as he walked soundlessly down to the second floor and approached his father's bedroom again. He opened the door all the way this time, slowly, quietly, and entered the room. He crept over to the bed, where his father still lay sleeping and snoring, looked down into his face, and then parted the curtains and looked out the window.

No car, no man.

He stood there for some time, watching. Afterward, he had no idea how long the window had held him there, peering into the yard. He couldn't recall how he had gotten out of the attic and back downstairs. All he remembered after standing silently above his father's sleeping form was sitting on the couch and staring through the front window at the empty yard until he fell asleep, wondering how to talk to his father about all this tomorrow.

5

DANE WOKE THE next morning to find his father sitting in his favorite armchair, inches from his head, watching him sleep. When he opened his eyes, he saw his father's face, upside down, smiling at him. He pushed away the blanket, sat up, and rubbed the heels of his hands into his eyes.

Snapping awake from such a short, fitful sleep took as much will as Dane could muster, but he determined to talk to his father before Sabine arrived later in the morning. *Who knows how long it might take to get anything useful out of him?* Dane thought. In his mind, he saw his father sitting there, staring through that window, laughing at whatever he saw down there, and still couldn't reconcile it with what he had seen last night. Maybe both of them were losing grip of reality.

"Morning, Pop," Dane said, pushing himself to his feet, feeling his spine crack all the way up to his neck. "Let's get you some breakfast."

Branson smiled up at him wordlessly but rose to his feet as soon as Dane touched his arm and he followed his son into the kitchen. After seating his father at the table, Dane went looking for something to eat. Within a minute of going back and forth from the fridge to the pantry to the cupboards, Dane regretted not packing some basic snacks along with his overnight bag and toiletries.

The easiest thing in there was cereal and milk, but the only type of cereal was those soft and soggy ones that made for easy, tasteless eating. Taking out two bowls, Dane filled them both with some high-bran flakes and poured on the milk. As soon as the milk hit the flakes, they turned into mush.

"Best I can do."

Branson grinned and took the bowl from him, digging in as soon as it hit the table in front of him.

"Hey, Pop," Dane said, once his father slowed down his eating, "have you ever seen an old black car parked in front of the house overnight? I mean, really old, like from the forties or fifties? Classic? Vintage?"

"I like cars, but the doctor says I can't drive anymore," Branson said between mushy mouthfuls. "I'm a good driver, though."

Dane took a bite of his cereal, swallowed it without chewing, and then pushed the bowl away from himself. "Right, but an old black car? Like in the movies?"

"We used to take the car to the drive-in, your mother and me. You went with us sometimes."

Dane gritted his teeth and pulled out his phone. After running an image search for "cars from the forties and fifties," he swiped through pictures until he found one that looked the most like the one he had seen the night before. He enlarged the image as much as his screen would allow and then held it in front of his father's face.

"Do you know a car like this?"

Branson took the phone and showed it back to Dane, beaming. "That's my father's car, your grandpa's car." He looked at it again. "Pontiac Streamliner. The only one on the street. This one is the newer model. You can tell from the grill."

"Oh yeah?"

Dane took the phone back and looked at the picture again. He had known it wasn't the same car, probably couldn't have picked the exact right one if he had tried, but, surprisingly, his father could hone in on such a minor detail, even remembering the model of the car.

"He loved that car. Made me wash it every weekend, but he never let me drive it. But I'm a good driver."

A powerful light burned in Branson's eyes, an energy Dane hadn't seen for a while, even before his mother died. He wondered how long his father had been like this, how long it might last, and why he was just now noticing the difference.

"I took it one time, you know." Branson leaned over the table and hushed his voice. "Took the keys after Dad was asleep and pushed it down the street before I started the engine. Not joyriding, really. I took your mom on a date. We went to the drive-in. We saw *The Day the Earth Stood Still.* Your mom didn't like it, though."

More words poured out of Branson than Dane had heard his father speak in years. He couldn't remember having a conversation with his father that didn't lead to one of them annoyed or angry with the other. A spell had been cast over them, and Dane tried not to move or speak too much for fear of breaking it.

"She didn't like sci-fi movies, Pop?"

"She loved sci-fi movies. She loved all movies." Branson shook his head, suddenly very serious. "She didn't like it when she found out how I took the car. She was right. Dad was waiting up for me when I got home. I got a beating for it that night."

Dane smirked as he stirred the cereal around in his bowl. "I mean, you did steal the car," he said. "You had to see that beating coming."

Dane tried to keep a humorous tone, but the mention of beatings broke through to his core. He remembered the quick pull of his father's belt and the times he had felt the end of it, some he knew he deserved, and some he believed he didn't. Specifically, he remembered the last time his father had used a belt on him, and he pushed the thought away. He had only met his grandfather once before he died, even though for years Grandpa lived in an old folk's home in the same state, but he bet his father got his proficiency with the belt honestly.

"I didn't really care." Branson shrugged, smiling like a mischievous child. "I got beatings all the time back then. Might as well get one for having fun."

Dane had to appreciate the logic there. He looked back at the picture of the car on the phone. He tried to imagine his father washing it or his parents sitting in it at the drive-in movies, sci-fi playing on the screen while his mother sat there with her arms folded the way she always did to express her disapproval.

"Pop," he said nervously, "when was the last time you saw this car?"

Branson wrinkled his nose and laughed at him as if Dane had said the silliest thing.

"It's my father's car. I see it all the time."

Dane dropped his eyes to the mush in his bowl. Just like that, the spell broke, and Dane wondered if they were really having a moment, or if he had just gotten sucked into his father's delusion.

The door lock spun open, and the alarm dinged to announce someone opening the front door. Dane looked down the hall and saw Sabine walking through with her tote bag over her shoulder.

"*Bonjou*," she sang out as she entered the kitchen. "How was the sleepover?"

Dane stiffened, and a shock went through his mind. Did she know?

"Good," he answered tentatively. "Good. Pop slept all through the night. Didn't even seem to need me."

Sabine set her bag on the counter, walked over to Branson, and kissed him on the cheek, and then Dane. She picked up Branson's bowl and looked at Dane, gesturing with her eyes to ask if he wanted more. Dane answered by sticking his tongue out in an expression of disgust. She carried both bowls to the sink and washed them.

"If you're taking over, I'm going to do some stuff in the attic," Dane said.

Sabine dried the bowls and put them away without turning to look at him. "I thought you had finished everything up there?"

"I thought so too, but something came up," Dane said. "You know what I mean?" He watched her face intently, like a seasoned poker player, hunting a tell.

Sabine nodded. "Something always does." She sat at the table with Branson. "No worries. Everything is under control here."

Dane turned and walked up the stairs. It felt crazy, what he was thinking, imagining, what he expected to see up there. He felt more and more stupid with every step he took as if someone were going to yell "gotcha" and point a camera at him. He felt tired, groggy even, and the thoughts in his head were like a fresh puzzle dumped out the table.

Still, he knew he had seen that car last night, his father walking to it, sitting in it. Or could it have been his grandfather? He didn't know him well enough to be sure. He had seen pictures of him, and they did resemble one another. He and Branson had the same build, the same height. In a lot of ways, they looked like the same man.

Dane paused in front of the attic door, worried about what he might see through that window, worried he might see nothing at all, worried about what seeing these things would mean about him. He had just turned forty-seven, on the downward slope toward fifty, with a family history of Alzheimer's and dementia.

If his father's mind was so far gone at eighty-five, then how long would it be before he started to show signs himself? The fear of his own mind, more than any curiosity, forced him to open the door and take another look. He needed to prove to himself that, no matter how crazy it seemed, the crazy was through the window and not inside himself.

He moved the broom and the other traps out of the way and set a crate in front of the window. Before even sitting down, he could see the old black Pontiac sitting by the curb, and that dizzy feeling returned. Once he had settled onto the crate and leaned forward a bit, he could see two figures in the yard. The first was the man he had seen last night.

In the light of day, he could see it was clearly not his father, but the similarities were so striking that Dane still had difficulty shaking the connection. The other figure was a boy, about ten, wearing jeans with the cuffs rolled up a bit, making a crisp white circle around his ankle, like Dane had seen in some of the faded photos from his father's childhood.

He couldn't hear anything, even when the two were obviously talking to each other, and he didn't know what would happen if he opened the window, but he watched the father and son, his grandfather and father, in their silent play in the front yard. They both had on their baseball gloves, and Grandfather mimed the large sweeping movement of an outfielder throwing the ball all the way to second. He did it several times, each time more intense than the last, and his body had the fluid grace of an dancer.

Dane hadn't known his grandfather very well, had never spent much time with him, had never heard many stories, and so the simple game of catch outside mesmerized him, as if watching the history of his clan filled an empty spot in him.

But underneath the feeling of curiosity flowed a deep sense of envy. He watched as his grandfather lobbed the ball to the ten-year-old boy who would grow up to be his father, and he couldn't help feeling jealous. He didn't have many memories of his father playing with him, even though his Branson had always been an athlete. The way he remembered it, Branson just shouted criticism across the court, and then after one last losing game, one last fight, he never showed interest again.

The boy downstairs in the rolled-up jeans kept dropping the ball, and the man kept showing him how to do it. The man's face cringed every time the boy threw the ball short and made him have to practically dive to catch it, or sideways into the bushes, making him have to dig around through the thorny branches for it.

There was so much difference between the man's effortless grace and the boy's clumsy, artless throwing that Dane wondered about all the stories he had heard regarding his father's sports abilities; all those memories passed on to him by his mother, who had watched him through high school; all those trophies and pennants his father had shown him growing up, instead of actually playing with him.

Every time the man retrieved the ball from whatever inconvenient place the boy threw it, he grew visibly angrier. His demonstrations turned into mockeries. Like a dark sky threatening storm, his expression transformed from earnest and serious to dark and vexed. Frustration dripped from his face with his sweat.

After a dozen or more of the boy's failed attempts to throw straight and get the ball anywhere near the glove, the father yelled a noiseless diatribe at him for more than a minute. His body contorted into the weakest imaginable caricature of the child's frame and then into the quintessential posture of an MLB pitcher.

The man's eyes narrowed as his arm cocked back, and then his arm vanished in lightning fast movement as it swung in its arc. He released the ball, and Dane watched as the boy made a weak attempt to get his glove up to catch it.

The ball struck the boy flush on the right side of his forehead, just above his eye, so hard his whole head snapped back, so hard that Dane felt a sympathetic pain in his own skull. Stumbling backward from the force of the blow, the boy lost his footing and crumpled onto the lawn.

Across from him, the man yelled again, his mouth wide, his arms pumping up and down, commanding the boy to get up. The boy tried, got to one knee, and then toppled over in a dizzy heap.

The man shouted one last thing, snatched the baseball glove off his hand, chucked it at the boy lying sideways on the grass with his head in his hands, and stomped his way into the house. Dane winced, expecting to hear the door slam, but the harsh silence was worse than whatever noise he imagined.

The boy tried one more time to get to his feet, cradling the right side of his head with one hand as he pressed the other into the ground to steady himself. Apparently giving up, he slumped back into a seated position with his head between his knees.

Dane watched as the boy sat there wordlessly, two abandoned gloves near him on the ground, his trembling hands covering the back of his head. Then a woman came through the front door and walked toward the boy with a bowl in her hands. Dane could only see her from the back, but the figure and the tall hair-sprayed mass of perfect brown hair matched every photo he had ever seen of his grandmother.

She had died before Dane was born, but Branson had told him countless stories about her and had shown him so many pictures that he knew almost everything about her, and virtually nothing about his grandfather. She knelt beside the boy, placed the bowl on the ground, and stroked the back of his head until he looked up at her. Tears made pink tracks through the dirt on his face, and already a darkening lump swelled over his eye on the right side.

The woman kissed his forehead gently and took a small piece of steak from the bowl on the ground. She knelt next to him, her left hand around his shoulder, her right pressing the cold meat to the flesh of his forehead. Within a minute, the boy nodded, and she helped him to his feet. He took the meat from her, held it to his own head, and stepped into her embrace. She patted the back of his head and then turned to walk him back into the house.

When she turned around to come back in, Dane saw her face more clearly, the same round face with beautiful high cheeks and the perfect smile he had seen in the picture still hanging in the living room downstairs. He also saw the bruise covering her entire left eye socket, a dark purple that contrasted with the brightness of her skin in the sunlight. The mother and son leaned on each other as they walked into the house.

Dane stared into the empty yard until the sunlight made bright spots at the top of his field of vision. He blinked a few times, but the spots were still there. He had never known his grandfather in any real way and had always resented the time his friends spent with their grandparents.

Branson used to visit Dane's grandfather in the old folks' home once a month. His mother would plan some games for the two of them until Branson returned, but he couldn't understand why he we wasn't allowed see his grandfather like other kids, why they couldn't all go together.

When he asked why he couldn't go, his father told him Grandpa was getting too old to have kids around, and too much commotion and noise upset him. Even then, the answer didn't satisfy him, and he had always wondered what kind of grandfather didn't like kids.

Suddenly, he didn't want to be near the attic anymore. Walking downstairs, the image of that boy curled up on the lawn wouldn't leave his mind. He turned the corner into the living room, and saw the same face looking up at him from his father's favorite chair, grinning the same way the boy had when he had thrown that first ball several feet short.

The old man didn't say a word, just watched Dane attentively as he walked around the back of the couch and sat at the end next his chair. In his father's eighty-five-year-old face, Dane could still see the boy, still see the darkening knot, still see the confused mixture of guilt and sadness and love sitting on the lawn, probably wondering why he couldn't throw straight, probably determined to be the best outfielder ever so his dad wouldn't be mad at him.

The old man, still grinning, still watching, slipped his hand over his son's hand on the arm of the couch as Dane stared away into nothing, gritted his teeth, and held back the pity and sadness shaking his shoulders.

6

SABINE TOOK BRANSON out for his afternoon walk, and Dane tried to get some work done on the couch, flanked by books and papers, his computer on his lap. Instead of planning lessons for the coming school year, his mind kept returning to the sight of his grandfather as a younger man, trying to reconcile it with the memory of the last time he had seen him alive.

Dane had one real memory of his grandfather. A forgotten afternoon from the spring of fifth grade came back to him now that he was alone with his thoughts in the house where he grew up, distracted by the sight of the crumpled boy and his grandmother's black eye.

Ever since Dane could remember, Grandpa had lived alone in an apartment building with lots of other old people.

"So," Dane asked tentatively from the backseat of the car, "there's no kids living there, like, at all?"

"No," Branson said in a clipped tone. "The building doesn't even allow kids to live there, just to visit." He glanced over his shoulder at Dane and met his eyes for just a moment, "And Grandpa doesn't like having kids around anyway."

As young as he was then, Dane couldn't help feeling confused and a little hurt. He didn't know his grandfather well enough to miss him, or even feel slighted by the rejection, but the idea that his own grandfather didn't to see him, probably would find him annoying, went against everything he knew about family. None of the movies he had watched of the stories his friends had told prepared him for this.

"But, Pop," Dane said, still trying to sort it all out in his head, "What about when you were little? Didn't Grandpa like kids then?"

Dane saw his father's eyes flash his way in the rearview mirror, but he didn't answer. At least a minute passed, the car softly rumbling toward its destination.

Then Branson cleared his throat. "No," he answered. "Not really."

Dane watched his father, waiting for an explanation, a story, something, but none came. Instead, he saw his mother reach over and rest her hand on his father's shoulder, rub it gently and squeeze his arm, the way she would caress Dane's own arm whenever he would fidget in church or get upset at a scary movie. Dane watched for a moment more, then played his Game Boy for the rest of the silent ride.

At ten, it seemed like a long drive. He had no real concept of the distance, but it always ran down the batteries in his Game Boy when they went for a visit to Grandpa. But he did understand that the word *visit* didn't really describe these trips. Every time, except once, they would drive the entire way, park outside the double doors of the building lobby. Branson said goodbye and walked inside, and then Dane's mother would slide into the driver's seat.

"Ready for our date?" she would sing to him, while his father waved goodbye and walked into the old folks' home.

Then came a cherished routine, a special adventure with mom. She would take him to Chuck E. Cheese nearby, and they would spend all afternoon there. He loved those times with his mother, especially because she would play the games with him, rolling the balls next to him in the Skee-Ball game or coaching him through the levels of Galaga, placing her fingertips on the screen where the next wave of bugs would appear. His father would take him sometimes, but he generally sat in a booth with a newspaper and a pizza while Dane played games and collected tickets. He looked forward to those afternoons alone with Mom, but he still wondered why only his father got to spend time with Grandpa.

On one of those afternoons, his parents had him dress up for the trip. He felt uncomfortable in his shirt, tie, and slacks. Nothing ever fit him comfortably. He had shot up three or four inches just since school had started, but he still had sort of a pot belly. His pants never seemed to find his shoes anymore, and his shirts constantly sneaked out of his waist, no matter how many times he tucked them in. He asked why he couldn't just wear shorts or jeans, and his parents told him it was a special day—Grandpa's birthday.

Mom promised that if he got dressed quickly enough and fixed his hair, they would let him carry the cake to the car. Dane raced through his bath and snatched on his clothes, driven by the round layer cake iced in white with blue edging and the number seventy on the top in fancy script. Instead of playing games, they told him they were going to have dinner at Grandpa's favorite restaurant. Dane remembered feeling a little disappointed that he would be missing out on spending alone time with his mother and playing video games, but the cake more than made up for it.

They picked up Grandpa at his apartment building and drove to the restaurant, mom in the back with Dane. Grandpa sat quietly in the passenger seat, arms folded in front of him. Dane held the cake carefully in his lap like his mother had told him, his arms wrapped around the box. The silent old man's face fascinated him, and he kept peeking around the car seat to get a look. He looked a lot like the photographs on the wall going down the staircase, but he had grown a bushy, gray beard. Once, Grandpa turned around just enough to see Dane and make eye contact. Dane smiled and giggled a little, but the old man just shook his head and turned back to look at the street ahead.

When they arrived, they entered a log cabin of a restaurant, decorated completely in dark brown wood, with picnic tables inside. The walls were covered with pictures of different kinds of gruff men fishing or chopping wood or the stuffed heads of deer and bears. A blackboard just inside the door advertised the special of the day, just the way Dane's teacher wrote the homework on the chalkboard. On the way to the table, a Pac-Man game tucked away against the wall caught Dane's attention. Instead of a stand-up cabinet, it was a table-top one you could sit down and play. Dane had never seen one before.

He pulled his mother's arm until she bent down to him. "Can I play?" he whispered, pleading with his eyes.

Mom stroked his back and said, "Maybe later." Even at ten, Dane knew what that really meant.

He didn't get too disappointed, though, because, in a moment, they sat at the table, and his mom told him to set the cake down, gently, in the middle. He wanted a slice of the cake at least as much as he wanted to play the arcade game.

Grandpa sat across from Dane but still hadn't spoken since they picked him up. He just perched there on the picnic table bench, with his hands folded in front of him as he had in the car. Dane remembered wondering how Grandpa could be so grumpy in such a cool place, supposedly his favorite restaurant. The atmosphere had immediately captivated Dane, and he started concocting ways to get his mother to bring him here instead of Chuck E. Cheese for their next date. The way it looked reminded Dane of someplace cowboys would eat after a long ride, except for the video game in the corner. So why was Grandpa just sitting there with his arms folded and his eyes squinted in a wrinkled frown?

As they ordered, Dane asked his father if they were going to have the cake after dinner.

Grandpa barked, "You want cake, kid?"

Dane beamed at his grandfather, excited to hear him talk, probably for the first time he could remember. "Cake is the best."

"You don't need any cake. You're too fat."

In Dane's memory, the entire room melted at the edges, and his grandfather's face, glowering down at him, filled the space. He had searched Grandpa's face for any sign of a joke, but could find no humor there, only the same squinted eyes he saw in some of the bigger boys at school, the ones who bullied him and his friends when they crossed paths before and after school. A look that never joked and only laughed when someone was hurt. A face full of something Dane couldn't quite identify, couldn't relate to, but felt hot and powerful and dangerous.

"You eat too much," Grandpa said, and Dane saw his father stretch out his hand and grip the old man's shoulder. Dane thought the look in his father's eye was the same one he gave Dane whenever he missed a free throw in a game or brought home a bad report card.

Dane remembered how hot his eyes felt, balancing next to his mother on the backless bench of the picnic table. He remembered how much he didn't want to cry in front of his father. Some years before, he had learned never to cry in front of him. Still, he felt the relentless eyes of everyone in the restaurant looking at him, laughing, and he couldn't understand why he was so wrong.

His mother took his hand in hers, under the table, just the tips of his fingers in hers. She rubbed his fingertips, but instead of making him feel better, he felt his shoulders shake on their own.

"Is he gonna cry now?" Grandpa said, looking from Dane to his father and back. "You gonna cry now, kid?"

In Dane's memory, it seemed as if the two things happened at the same time. On one side of the table, his father slapped the surface with his large, flat hand hard enough to resound through the entire restaurant and make the silverware at each setting jump an inch in the air and clatter back to the wood. On the other side, his mother drew her purse from where it sat on the bench next to her in one hand and pulled Dane's hand with the other. In one motion, they were on their feet together and walking away from the table, their backs turned to the two men with the striking resemblance, the same creased brow and wrinkled frown.

"Let's go check out that Pac-Man game," his mother whispered in his ear as they walked, rummaging in her purse for quarters. By the time they reached the tabletop game, she pinched a stack six of them between her index finger and thumb. She spread them on the glass top of the arcade game, smoothed Dane's hair, and gently pushed him down into the seat. Then she pulled the other chair opposite him and plopped the quarters into the slot, all six at once.

Dane wasn't very good at Pac-Man, but it took his mind off his grandfather for a while. He had never noticed before, but while it always took him at least two lives to clear the first screen, his mother almost always got to the second, once even the third, on one life. By the time the last credit disappeared from the bottom of the screen, the old man's words and eyes had lost most of their heat and noise in Dane's mind, and he felt better.

He looked up from watching his mother play her last life to see his grandfather walking past them, towards the door, holding a white box of food to go. The old man looked straight ahead, and Dane craned his neck to see him as he stepped outside and turned out of view. Then Branson walked up to them with a white plastic bag holding three more to-go boxes. He knelt down beside them and set the food on the corner of the game, trying not to block the screen.

"Who's winning?" he asked, cheerfully enough, but looking back, Dane remembered the odd deepness in his voice, a throaty rasp he normally only had after coaching a basketball game.

His mother let go of the joystick, and Pac-Man hit a wall and then exploded in a little starburst of yellow as two ghosts cornered him. She leaned across the game and kissed his father on one cheek, rubbing the stubble on the other side with her fingers.

They dropped Grandpa off at his apartment building, and he shuffled into the lobby by himself, with the white box of his favorite barbeque nestled in the bend of his arms. Dane remembered his father waiting just long enough to see the old man open the glass door to the lobby before pulling away, and his mother didn't even switch seats like she normally would. Instead, she sat in the back with Dane, taking turns playing Tetris on his Game Boy until the battery finally died.

When they got home, his mother opened the box and set the untouched cake on the kitchen counter. She drew a long, flat knife from the block and carefully scraped the top of the number seventy from the icing, leaving a number ten instead, with just a shallow indentation and the lightest smear of blue above the one. After they heated the boxed food, barbeque chicken and ribs, with sides of slaw and corn, they let Dane cut the cake into lopsided slices and serve everyone a piece.

Sitting there on the couch in the same house, the entire event came rushing back to him. It felt as if he might turn around and see the white take-out boxes and the cake still on the table. Dane couldn't figure out how he had forgotten that dinner. It was the last time he had seen his grandfather alive, and the memory of his harsh words made him feel as small and ashamed as when it happened. Even at Grandpa's funeral a couple of years later, he told his father he didn't want to see Grandpa, not in a coffin, but really, he just didn't want to look at the old man's sour face and pretend to feel sad. His father let him stay in his seat and look through a comic book until the end of the service.

How could he have forgotten that day? Looking back on it, he could see his father stepping in to defend him, but he had completely missed it at the time and then promptly forgotten about it.

As he sat there on the couch, lost in this memory, the front door opened, and Branson stepped through with Sabine right behind him. Branson stopped just inside the house, staring and smiling down at Dane. His face practically throbbed bright red from the sun and the exertion. Sabine pressed him a little farther inside and closed the door behind him, slipping into the kitchen and leaving the two men in silent contemplation of each other.

Something about his father's face struck Dane in a way he had never noticed before. It wasn't the smile nor the flush in the cheeks. Dane had seen his father get excited after coaching a game or exhausted after playing one, and he had worked hard as a child to see his smile, often without success. Something about that last memory of his grandfather still hung in the air.

His father was about the same age now as his grandfather had been when he died, and they looked almost exactly alike. They could have been the same man if Branson had only let himself grow a ragged white beard. It made Dane wonder how similar they were in other ways. He remembered his father barking at him with the same cutting tone and he could see where it came from. As a child it had always surprised him, until it didn't anymore. How much more of his grandfather lurked in his father somewhere, hidden away or sometimes let off the leash? How much of that old man survived in Dane himself?

7

LATER IN THE afternoon, Dane shaved his stubble and met Muriel for an early dinner before spending another night with his father. Even under normal circumstances, he hated being away from her for just one night, but this time it felt as if months had passed, and he had so much he wanted to tell her, and no idea how to begin. Walking into their apartment, Dane found Muriel's rice and brown beans on the table with a bag of salad and rotisserie chicken from the grocery store. Clearly a busy day if she had resorted to store-cooked chicken to save time.

Right after she met him at the door with a kiss, Muriel demanded a detailed update on his father's mental state. Dane smiled at her awkwardly, afraid to tell her everything that had gone on in the house, afraid she would question his mental state instead of the old man's.

It took ten minutes of eating in silence before Muriel asked, "Did you sleep alright?"

Dane paused and shook his head before putting his fork down.

"Your father kept you up? Or just a strange bed?"

"It's my bed, so it shouldn't be strange, but I slept on the couch. Pop slept fine, all through until morning."

He looked into her brown eyes, wanting so much to tell her about the window, but instead went back to his plate.

"So he's not that bad yet, I guess?"

"It's not good. Something is wrong," Dane said. "I don't even know how to describe it."

Muriel pushed away her almost empty plate, leaned her head into her hands, elbows on the table, and watched her husband. Experience had taught Dane that this was her way of making a quiet stand, making herself immovable. He looked at her and shrugged.

"Did something happen?" she asked.

Dane watched her eyes for a sign of readiness, a path to telling the impossible, a way to word it so he didn't sound crazy.

"I think I'm going to have to stay there for a while."

"Okay."

"We can't afford to come out of pocket for home care at night. His Medicare isn't going to pay for any more services. And . . ." Dane lifted his feet onto the rung of the dining chair and pressed his knees against the underside of the table. "I feel like I . . . *I* saw him a little last night."

Muriel's face brightened immediately. "That's great!" she said. "That's exactly what I prayed for last night, for both of you."

Dane chuckled nervously. "You must have a direct line then."

"Would you just tell me what happened?" Muriel slapped him across the shoulder.

"It's complicated." Dane leaned over and kissed her. "What would you think about moving in there with me, just for a while?"

Muriel kissed him back and squeezed his hand. "Of course!"

"Really?"

"Isn't that why we said we didn't want our own kids? So we could just pick up and go whenever we want to? So we could help people, with our time and our money, whenever they needed us? Absolutely. I don't want to stay in this house, or any house, without you anyway." She grabbed his face forcefully and kissed him several times. "I didn't sleep so well either last night."

Dane laughed at her, but then the smile melted from his face. "That's not why I was up last night."

"Okay," Muriel said, her face suddenly serious also.

"So, there's a window in the attic, just a little round window that looks out over the yard and the street. My father has just been sitting in front of it and staring outside, laughing and making all kinds of reactions."

Muriel took his hand and pressed it to her chest. "They get like that. My grandfather would sleep all the time and rest when he wasn't sleeping. He would stare at the television when it was off, just watch the wall and cry or laugh like he was remembering something and seeing it right in front of him."

Dane bit his lip the way he did when he held back his feelings, trying not to show any cracks. Muriel watched him, as if she were waiting for him to be ready.

"Did you ever see them too?" he said at last.

Muriel leaned back in her chair. "See what? See him staring?"

Dane shook his head. "His memories," he said softly. "I saw my father's memories too. I looked through the window, and I saw him when he was a kid. I saw my grandfather. I saw my grandmother."

"She died before you were born." Muriel slid her hands underneath her legs and sat up in her chair.

Dane explained what he had seen last night, the car, the game of catch, the dark circle of his grandmother's eye contrasting with her perfectly sprayed and set hair. Muriel watched him closely as he told it.

"Am I going crazy?" Dane asked, his voice breaking. "Am I going to be like him?"

"It's a lot," Muriel said, leaning forward and taking both of Dane's hands. "But I don't think it's crazy."

"You don't?"

Muriel held his hands still, but looked down at the table as though she was carefully preparing her words. "Your people have lived in that house for three generations now, and nobody else. Maybe all that life changes a place, sticks to it. We say we believe in spirits, in miracles," she said slowly. "We pray. And then something like this happens, and we just look away or refuse to accept it."

She collected the plates from the table, got up, and walked over to the sink. "My grandmother told me there was a place outside of the town where she grew up, a freshwater spring. She said you had to climb to get to it, but once you found it, it was like the rest of the world had disappeared. It was hot all year long, and if you stayed in the waters long enough, they would heal anything that was wrong with you.

"Grandmé said she went there when she was pregnant. She had started spotting and was worried she would lose another baby. She said she sat in that water for a few minutes and the spotting went away, and my mother was born about three months later." After dumping the plates into the sink, Muriel stood behind Dane, her hands on his shoulders, and bent over and kissed him on the head. "There have to be some magic places on the planet."

Dane turned his head up to her. "You really think so?"

She mussed his hair. "I don't think you're crazy, so there's that."

Dane grabbed her hand and kissed it. "Will you look through it with me?"

"No, *mesye,*" she answered immediately. She pulled him up from his chair and put a can of cleaning wipes in his hand before walking back to the sink. Dane pulled out a wipe and started cleaning the table, scooping crumbs and grains of rice into his left hand. "No way. Just because a place is magic doesn't mean it's good. Grandmé taught me that too."

After they cleaned the kitchen well enough to leave it for a couple of days, Muriel went upstairs and packed an overnight bag as fast as she could in order to get back to the old house and Branson before Sabine was set to leave.

Dane gathered some snacks from the pantry, some of his cookies and Muriel's organic trail mix, along with anything they didn't want to spoil in the fridge, and stuffed them into a cloth grocery bag. He set the bag in the back seat of his car and sat in the driver's seat, waiting for Muriel.

He had hoped to show her the window and prove that he wasn't hallucinating. *Maybe she'll change her mind,* he thought. But her words rattled him. He wondered if even he should look again. Not all magic places are good places.

The way his heart had raced in the middle of the night, the things he had seen there, the way his whole understanding of his family was shifting—what if it was all a trick? What if he wasn't crazy, but seeing things he shouldn't see could make him so? Should his father even be up there? What could it do to him? What had it already done?

Still, stronger than any of these fears, Dane felt a strong desire to look again, to see his father, to know him. Not just the man he had known growing up, but the boy who had become his father, the reasons why his father had turned out the way he did, why there was so much distance between them all his life.

If the window could help him see the man who raised him, then it couldn't be a bad thing. Every day now the old man slipped farther away from Dane, like an avalanche picking up speed and power, until it disappeared over the cliff. Soon, the old man would be gone forever, and any chance of knowing his father, reconciling with him, would vanish. But the *what-if* of it all filled him with a debilitating apprehension.

Ultimately, his caution defeated his curiosity, and he locked the attic door. After rummaging around in one of the kitchen drawers and trying every spare key in it, one of them finally fit the attic lock. He told himself he was locking it to keep his father from wandering up there and hurting himself, but he knew he was doing his best to resist the window's call himself. He decided if Muriel wouldn't look, then maybe he shouldn't either, even though a powerful part of him wanted to. The most important thing to him was that she was with him, helping him taking care of his father and everything else.

One more month of summer remained, just four weeks before professional development meetings for both of them, before they had to submit lesson plans online and prepare classrooms to receive students.

Dane and Muriel took a couple of days to move in just enough of their clothes and other comforts so they could stay with Branson for the entire month, working on their computers downstairs while Sabine tended to Branson during the day and then putting all the work away and taking over care of the old man by early evening.

The attic would have been a much quieter and more out-of-the-way place for him and Muriel to work, but she wouldn't go near it, and he told her he didn't want the distraction himself. Though whether the right word was *distraction* and not *temptation* was something he debated for the first few days as they settled in. He didn't tell her that he had decided to stay away.

Sabine came through the front door with a red-faced and sweaty Branson after a walk around the neighborhood, which she did every day around noon.

"You should have seen your father," she cooed like a kindergarten teacher lauding her pupil. "We went all the way around the block, the long way, twice." She emphasized the point with a gentle rub of Branson's shoulder and two ecstatic fingers in the air. "Mr. Branson even jogged a little when the neighborhood ladies passed by."

Branson beamed and flexed a bit as he shuffled slowly to the bathroom, clearly losing steam.

Once he turned the corner out of earshot, Sabine leaned in towards Dane, her eyes still on Branson until he closed the bathroom door.

"I'm just trying to get his appetite up," she said unashamedly. "He hasn't been eating much for the past few weeks, but he should have a good lunch today and sleep well for you tonight." She snapped her fingers in self-congratulation. "You're welcome."

The next day, Muriel put down her work to join Sabine and Branson on their walk. She cajoled Dane to put away his computer as well and practically dragged him outside with the rest of them.

Up to the first bend, Muriel walked arm in arm with Dane, but after a short distance in sulky silence, she reached up and kissed him on his cheek, then trotted ahead to join Sabine. Together, the four of them made a little cross moving up the sidewalk, Branson strutting in front, Sabine and Muriel girl-talking in Creole behind him, and Dane hanging back, pondering the scene unfolding in the neighborhood.

The younger couples and families were all gone to work, but enough retired folks still populated the suburb to create a meager audience for Branson's procession. Some of the men were out mowing or watering their lawns, and they stopped long enough to send manly greetings his way.

"Watch out now, Branson," one elderly man hollered over his edger's engine.

Dane watched his father salute them or wave and point in some secret masculine code. A streak of envy ran through Dane's heart, watching the easy way these men all communicated, compared with how awkward and insecure he always was around his own father. *If they only knew him like I do*, he thought.

Around the block, on the return trip, Branson flagged a bit, his step losing some of its bounce and his stride closing nearly to a shuffle. But when a couple of old ladies, apparently sisters, left their gardens and adjusted their floppy, wide-brimmed hats to sing "Good morning, Branson," in two-part alto harmony, his step magically quickened. His shoulders tossed back, and the enthusiasm returned to his stride. Muriel and Sabine giggled and tapped each other's arms as they waved deferentially to the enchanted old ladies.

Dane watched the coquettish scene unfold and didn't realize he had stopped walking until the rest of his party nearly reached the next corner a few yards ahead. As he hustled to catch up, he waved to the ladies, trying to pin down memories of them as well as the other neighbors his father's age. Some of them had lived there since he was a boy, and in their own ways, had changed as much and as little as his father had changed.

Watching their interactions with his father amazed him. Everyone liked Branson, but Dane wondered if they would like him as much if they knew the things he knew about him. If they had lived with him during those years when his mother had to be both the bond and the buffer between them, would they see him the same way? Then again, when he went on those walks with Sabine and his father, he started to wonder the opposite. How would he see his father if he didn't have all that history blocking his view?

When the four of them walked back into the house, they wordlessly split up and each went about their own business. Branson headed straight for the bathroom, while Sabine went to the kitchen to prepare his lunch. Muriel pulled her papers, books, and laptop together and sat down to work, surrounded by her sea of materials.

Dane, however, left them all behind and mounted the steps to the attic. He had seen a bit more of his father through others' eyes, people who viewed him as only the nice old man next door, and he burned to see more.

Dane unlocked the attic door, crouched by the window, and watched. There was nothing to see at first. No black Pontiac parked outside, nobody in the yard, but the dizzy sensation in his head made him hopeful. He looked across the street, but even the houses seemed quiet, almost deserted for what looked like midday.

He watched for a few minutes longer. Just as he started to thank the heavens that his weakness had been rewarded with disappointment, a car coming down the street registered in his periphery. He watched the familiar elegant black sedan float to the curb in front of the house.

A moment after the car stopped, Dane saw his father—perhaps thirteen years old—get out of the front passenger side and carefully shut the door behind him. He stood on the curb for a moment, scanning the grass as if he had lost something there. Then his father, Dane's grandfather, stepped out of the driver's seat and did the same.

The two of them dressed exactly alike in buttoned black suits with white shirts and shoes so polished Dane could see the shine from the attic window. He could also see his grandfather's face, and he recognized his strained expression in an instant. Dane had seen the same look before hundreds of times in the mirror. He felt every crease of skin and contraction of his grandfather's expression in the muscles of his own face. Earlier, he had thought his grandfather was the picture of his father, but at that moment, it felt more like his own face gazing up at the sky and away from the boy in the black suit still standing on the curb, still staring at the ground.

Neither one of them moved, and Dane knew why.

The look on his grandfather's face was the same look Dane had worn to his mother's funeral, biting his lip, bating his breath. It was the look of a man holding back a swarm of feelings that threatened to overtake and embarrass him, to break his carefully created mask and reveal his true self.

Muriel called it *the statue* when they first married, saying "I see the statue," whenever she caught Dane concentrating on emotional control. She stopped calling it that or calling attention to it at all after Dane had snapped at her a couple of times. Now she just let him be and left him alone to sort things out whenever this stoic way came over him.

The boy by the car was about thirteen. Grandma had died soon after Branson's thirteenth birthday. It was one of the hundreds of stories Branson had told Dane about her, one of the many proofs of her sainthood and a reminder of how much she and Dane's mother had in common.

The old man and the boy slowly made their way to the house and stood facing the door. As Dane watched the expression on grandfather's face tighten and close, just as he knew his own did from time to time, he saw his father, the young teenager beside him, finally move. He didn't step forward but just kept his eye on the ground and reached up to take his father's hand as they stood in front of the house. He folded his hand into his father's, and for just a moment, they stood there together, really together, connected through touch.

Then the man mashed the heel of his free hand into his eye socket, and his face tightened even more. He shook his other hand as if there were a mosquito or a wasp on it, and the boy let go. Once the man's hand was free, he swung it behind the boy's shoulder, and for a moment, it looked to Dane as if he were going to place it on his head, caress the cropped hair.

But instead, his large-knuckled hand came whipping forward and smacked the boy on the back of the head hard enough to make it snap forward and back. The man said something Dane couldn't hear, something short, mashed both hands into both eye sockets this time, and then walked to the house, leaving the boy standing on the sidewalk all alone.

Dane hated the man. He hated the look on the man's face, hated how it made him look darker and harder, somehow decades older and yet so damn childish at the same time. He hated the way the brute's face looked away from the boy behind him, the boy who lowered his head with the blush and shine of tears covering his cheeks.

He hated the fierceness and coldness in the eyes and the strain in the brow, the teeth threatening to bite right through the lower lip. And he hated knowing that the identical expression, every crease and scowl, was on his own face at the same time. He tried to relax his jaw, his eyes, to let himself feel, to let himself cry for the boy standing alone downstairs, but the tightness had a hold on him.

There was nobody in the room with him, nobody around to see, nobody there but himself, and still he couldn't let it out. Part of him said he wasn't like his grandfather. He wasn't mean; he would never do anything so cruel to his son. But another part reminded him that he didn't have a son, and that if his own wife, a good woman and kind, had given up trying to comfort him—or even talk to him when his face looked like chiseled marble—then how different could he be?

He turned away from the window and wanted to leave but had to relax first. He started with his eyes, then exhaled through pursed and rounded lips, like a slashed tire deflating until it rested on the ground. Once his eyes stopped burning and he could breathe normally again, he left the attic and closed the door behind him.

Night couldn't come quickly enough for Dane. After an early dinner out with Muriel, while Sabine took care of Branson, Dane helped his father get up to bed. The old man fell asleep in his chair, exhausted after an active day and a heavy meal. In the meantime, Muriel took her things to the bathroom to bathe and settle down for the night.

Branson practically flopped into bed, dropping back with his feet over the side and then slowly dragging in one foot after the other. Dane pulled the blanket up to his father's waist, turned to leave, and then looked back down at him.

"What was Grandma like?" he asked his father as he softly sat next to him on the bed.

Branson shifted onto his side and mumbled something sleepily, looking at Dane through lidded eyes.

"What was that?"

Branson rubbed his eyes with the heels of his hands with the same movement Dane had seen his grandfather make on the lawn. "She was beautiful." Branson strained to speak louder. "She always took such good care of me and protected me."

"Protected you from what?" Dane asked, but Branson's eyes were closed, and he didn't respond. After adjusting the blanket a little to compensate for his father's shifting body, Dane got up and slipped out of the room, slowly closing the door behind him until he heard the faintest click of the doorknob.

He set his ear against the door and listened for his father's snoring to start. While he stood there, silently leaning in and completely focused, he imagined his grandmother doing the same thing at the same door, listening to him, looking out for him. Did she wait for him to go to sleep too? Did she cover for him when his father was in one of those rages? Did she get that black eye because she knew the anger in her husband was still boiling, and she didn't want her son to get burned any worse by it?

But one question both intrigued and horrified him long after he crept away from the bedroom door: *Who protected Branson after his mother died?*

8

"I CAN'T SLEEP in this bed," Muriel whispered in the dark of night. Dane adjusted his body next to her and pulled her closer, but it didn't mean much on such a narrow bed. Dane's back pressed against the cold wall of his old bedroom, and if they moved much farther apart, Muriel would flop out of the bed onto the floor.

"I can't get comfortable," she hissed, writhing next to Dane. Her warm thighs slid against hi, in a way that would have meant something entirely different in their own home and their own bed. Dane stifled a laugh and buried his face in the back of Muriel's neck.

"It's not funny," Muriel said bucking Dane off with a shake of her shoulders. "There's something hard in the bed. It keeps rubbing up against my hip."

Dane's left arm, draped over her midsection, slid under the hem of her t-shirt, and lightly gripped the rise of her hip. "You want me to rub it somewhere else," he whispered in her ear.

Pushing his hand away, Muriel sucked her teeth and crossed her arms in front of her. "I'm trying to sleep."

"You started it," Dane chuckled, but kept his hands to himself. He knew she was right; the bed really was too small for the two of them to sleep in, by at least half. Without even seeing her face in the dark room, he felt her annoyance in the rigidness of her muscles.

"I'm not starting anything," Muriel growled, "I'm about to end it. I could sleep better on the couch by myself."

"No, babe," Dane cooed, rubbing Muriel's bare arm. "I missed you."

Muriel uncrossed her arms, but her stiff posture didn't soften much. "I missed you, too," she muttered.

"You did start it, though," Dane said, tentatively, "when you walked in here with your bags this afternoon. You took one look at the bed and went on about how I'd have to hug you up all night, how delighted you would be, sleeping in my arms again like when we first got married."

"Delighted," Muriel sneered.

"You literally said *delighted*." Dane carefully, lightly slid his hand back under her shirt onto her bare hip. When she didn't push it away this time, he let its weight rest against her.

"That's because I was thinking about hugging instead of sleeping," she said, the tension in her voice dissipating with each word, "we never hug in the bed at night anymore."

"C'mon," Dane whispered, close to Muriel's ear, "never?"

"*Janmen*," she whispered back, twisting her head to avoid his lips. "Never." She rolled slightly onto her back, peering upward into his eyes, her shoulder just over the edge of the mattress. "Ever since we got that king bed, no more hugging. Just you on your side across the room, reading and playing games on that thing."

"It's a console," Dane said flatly, resisting the direction the conversation was headed.

"I hope it consoles you," Muriel snapped, "because it annoys the heck out of me."

"You wanted the king bed," Dane responded. "You said you wanted more space."

"Not space between *us*," Muriel retorted, "space for sleeping, space for hugging, space for . . ."

Her voice trailed off.

Dane rested his hand on her belly, above her navel, and made tiny smooth circles on her skin. "Space for what?" He smiled.

Muriel slapped his hand and shoved it against his leg.

"I'm serious," she said.

Dane looked closely at her in the dark, and her eyes seemed bigger, brighter, somehow.

"I miss our . . ."—Muriel's voice broke softly—"intimacy."

Dane perched on his elbow as much as he could and leaned over her face, scanned her eyes in the dark. She turned her head away from him towards the far side of the room, and her shoulders shuddered, once, and then again against his chest.

"We're intimate," he said plaintively, "more than most people, more than any of our friends, with kids sneaking in the bed all hours of the night."

"That's not intimacy," Muriel shook her head, "I really do miss you." She looked up at him, her black eyes even brighter now in the dark room. She reached out with her open hand and found his upper arm, gripped it as if afraid of tumbling off the bed. "I miss falling asleep in your arms, waking up with you next to me." Her voice hitched, and her nails dug into Dane's arms. "I used to feel so safe. I want to sleep like that again."

Dane clumsily felt his way along her neck and cupped her face, felt hot tears on her cheek.

"I knew we couldn't make love in this room," Muriel went on, leaning into Dane's touch, "I knew it would be weird and awkward."

"Yeah," Dane huffed.

Muriel pulled her head away.

Dane drew his hand back.

"I thought we would have to sleep all cuddled up together, like we used to, like when we first got married, and you don't get it, and now I can't even sleep."

"I do get it," Dane whispered.

"I can't remember the last time I felt your heartbeat."

Muriel turned over, her back towards Dane. He felt her shoulder press against his chest, her hips against his thighs. Slipping his right hand underneath her waist, with his left he threaded his fingers into her curls.

Muriel jerked away from him and sat up on the edge of the bed. The lamp on the nightstand snapped on, filling the room with harsh light.

"I'm going downstairs to read until I get sleepy," she said.

Dane withdrew his hand and watched as she eased forward, reaching for her tablet, but then settled back onto the bed. From the nightstand, she stroked the edge of the stack of greeting cards Dane had kept from the trash heap of his mother's old things. Picking up the top one, she opened it, revealing the wedding ring taped inside, his mother's thin but ornate band.

"Hmm," Muriel laughed, circling the edge of the ring with her fingertip as she read the inside of the card.

Dane sat up in the bed and shifted his legs across the mattress so that he sat next to his wife with his back against the wall, careful not to touch her.

"So like her," Muriel said, wiping her face with the shoulder of her t-shirt. Smiling, she traced the words on the cards as if they were written in braille. "That woman could turn her love into ink."

Dane nodded. "She was the best."

Muriel laid the card with the wedding ring to the side of the stack and picked up the next one, opening it gingerly. "Every day grows sweeter," she read, the last word lost in her laughter.

"Not exactly poetic, right?" Dane said.

Muriel shrugged. "It's enough." She caressed the velvet cover with her fingertips.

"Did I ever tell you about the note she left for me on our wedding day?" Muriel said, laying aside the Valentine and turning to look at Dane.

Dane shook his head.

"It was on the mirror in my dressing room at the church, stuck on the side right where I would have to see it." Muriel smiled, but her voice faltered and she quickly covered her mouth with her palm. "My daughter, you are beautiful, thank you for bringing such light and life to our family."

Muriel's tears came so suddenly that Dane nearly leaped forward to put him arm around her shoulder, but she waved him back, resting her hand on his knee instead.

"I miss her," Muriel stammered through her tears.

Dane's eyes burned and he pressed the back of one hand into his eyes to blot his tears, his other hand covering Muriel's.

"I'm going downstairs to read," she said, pulling her hand away. Once on her feet, Muriel grabbed her tablet from the nightstand where it lay charging and slipped into the hallway.

Dane watched her leave the room, and his gut churned with regret. He hated arguing, but he hated this even more, this tension that never quite turned into an argument but turned the space between them into a rift, a canyon with no bridge. Standing, he steeled himself to walk downstairs and apologize for some offense he couldn't name and didn't understand.

Tired and confused, he walked down the stairs as quietly as he could testing each step with his toes before putting his weight on it. At the bottom, he turned into the living room, already rehearsing his confession in his head, but there was no one there.

He walked around the couch to see if Muriel might be lying down, just out of sight, but she just wasn't there. A glance over his shoulder into the kitchen showed him she wasn't there either.

Heading back up the stairs, cautiously, he saw Muriel at the top, and a soft light washed over her. A pleasant yellowish gleam cut a band through the open attic door and spilled down the first three or four top steps in a way that didn't make sense. It felt like Moses looking at the burning bush for the first time, something so simple and ordinary and yet somehow so impossible. The band of light didn't come all the way down the stairs, but it would have to bend at least twice just for him to see it.

When he crept up to the attic landing, Muriel walked through the doorway, bathed in the light streaming through the window. It fell across the floor in a narrow swath over the crates and ladder and through the door. Stepping inside, carefully, noiselessly, Dane watched as she walked to the window. He could see the night sky outside, and the light source was the street light outside the house.

Muriel sat on the crate in front of the window, and Dane quietly stood behind her. He saw a man standing under the street light. Not a man exactly, a teenaged boy, almost a man. He looked to be about sixteen or seventeen, tall and athletic. He looked exactly like his father in some of the family photos. Specifically, one photo Dane had seen a hundred times. It showed Branson at his physical peak, probably seventeen or eighteen, about the same age as the young man outside under the street light. In the photo, Branson had his shirt off and his basketball shorts on. The picture was taken after a game, and Branson was flexing his muscles in the exultation of a big win. Branson used to carry that photo around in his wallet and passed it around whenever the conversation turned even remotely to anything involving sports, fitness, or muscles—and even sometimes when it didn't.

Branson had stopped carrying it and showing it off some time ago, but Dane remembered it clearly and knew he was looking at the same young man down on the sidewalk, leaning against the streetlight and tracing a circle in the concrete with his white Converse sneakers.

Muriel reached to open the window, hesitated, and snatched her hand away. She seemed nervous, like an eavesdropper who could get caught any second. Dane empathized, feeling skittish himself, sneaking up behind his wife. He wanted to call out to her, but she had been so annoyed with him, and if he didn't know how she would react, him catching her up here.

Suddenly, the young Branson downstairs seemed to lose interest in the cracks in the sidewalk. He straightened up and focused his gaze down the street, like a pointer snapping to attention at the smell of a duck. Muriel leaned into the convex window, carefully, as if it might pull her through or trap her. Dane glided closer, as quietly as he could, but before he stopped, Muriel turned his way, her finger on her lips, eyes still focused on the window, and waved him over with her hand, patting the other crate beside her.

Dane sat down next to her, and a young woman came into view through the window—a pretty girl, tall and slim with an athletic build. Muriel instantly laughed out loud before clapping both hands over her mouth. The young woman stepped into the circle of light with young Branson, and his posture immediately went from cautiously alert to full-on preening, shoulders back and chest out. The pretty girl reached out to hug him, and it seemed as if all the rigidity drained from his body, as if his very bones softened. He hugged her back in the most awkward way possible, one hand pressed to her shoulder blade, the other hovering over the small of her back. Muriel giggled through her interlaced fingers.

"I thought you didn't want to see up here," Dane whispered. "I thought Grandmé said magic places aren't always good."

Startled out of her fascination for a moment, Muriel turned to look at him. She pressed her fingers to her lips. "Shut up," she hissed. "They're going to hear you."

Dane crouched next to her and put his arm around her shoulders.

"It's your mom," Muriel whispered and covered her mouth with her hand again, giggling uncontrollably.

Dane looked through the window and saw his father standing on the sidewalk under the streetlight next to a girl. They both looked extremely young and terribly nervous. Actually, young Branson looked more nervous, kicking at nothing in particular with white canvas sneakers a full two inches from the rolled cuffs of his jeans.

"They can't hear us, weirdo," Dane said.

"How do you know?"

"I guess I don't know," he said, shifting his weight to try to get comfortable before pulling up another crate next to Muriel's. "We can't hear them."

"Even if you open the window?"

Dane made his eyes big and shook his head slowly. He told her about his father trying to open the door and lean out.

"Enough said." Muriel tapped her temple. "I feel like I'm dancing with the devil up here as it is. I don't need any more temptation." She leaned over to Dane's ear and whispered, "I felt like something was pulling me up here. I still feel dizzy."

Dane squeezed her shoulders and nodded. "Are you sure that's Mom?"

Muriel slapped his arm and gestured out the window. "That is your mom," she said, pausing with each word. "Look at her. She's so pretty."

Dane looked. She really was pretty. He wondered if he and Muriel had a girl, how much she would look like his mother, and how much like hers. Would she look like the tall, athletic young woman on the sidewalk, somehow even taller in high-waisted jeans and a cardigan sweater that practically glowed pink under the streetlight?

Young Gwen had her eyes focused on young Branson, even though he looked everywhere but at her. He watched the ground, craned his neck to see through the windows of the house, watched up and down the street. At one point, he looked directly up at the attic window, and both Dane and Muriel ducked. Dane laughed, and Muriel crossed herself as they leaned toward the window again.

The young man downstairs said something to the pretty young woman, looking up at the stars as he said it. Whatever it was must have been effective because at the end of his speech, he reached out for the young woman's hand, and she folded her fingers into his. Muriel giggled and took Dane's hand in the same way. She nestled up to him under his arm.

After holding hands under the streetlight for a minute, young Branson finally looked down into the girl's eyes. She smiled, still holding his hand, and said something that brought the red into her cheeks.

Suddenly, both of the teenagers below snapped their heads in the direction of the house, as if something had exploded there and broken the spell of that lamplight. Their hands immediately separated, and Branson's face now burned dark red. He shouted something back at the house and then looked back down at the grass in front of him.

Muriel squeezed Dane's hand and looked up into his face, her eyes squinted and glassy. He pulled her close and gripped her shoulder. Downstairs, both teenagers were avoiding looking at each other as if a shower of embarrassment had doused the scene. Then, out of nowhere, Branson put his hand on the girl's shoulder, leaned in, and kissed her, quickly, just to the side of her lips.

Muriel covered her mouth to stop a squeal from filling the room and slapped Dane's leg six, seven, eight times.

Young Gwen, almost as tall as the athletic young man in the too-short jeans, brushed the mop of his brown hair away from his face, took his hand briefly once more, and then turned and walked down the street. Young Branson watched her until she turned the corner, and so did Dane and Muriel, both of their faces pressed against the convex glass of the window. Then the young man jogged into the house right below them.

Muriel pressed her forehead into Dane's chest for a minute, and he could feel the wetness of her tears through his shirt. She looked up at him, smiling pure joy as if she were the one falling in love that night. Dane smiled back at her, at her joy and the way the streetlight through the window brightened her face and her big brown eyes.

"Do you remember when we were like that?" Muriel asked, holding Dane's hand .

"We're still like that, aren't we?"

Muriel looked up at him, eyebrow cocked, and waggled her hand back and forth.

"Do you even remember the first time we met?" she asked.

"In the lounge at school," Dane answered, "you were trying to post a test on the system, and I helped you through it."

Muriel snatched her hand back and crossed her arms in front of her. "No," she snapped and then caught herself and lowered her voice. "No, that's not it."

"We were trying to get that test to work for a couple of hours," Dane retorted, "I had never been on that campus after four until that day. How can you not remember that?"

"No, we were chaperoning the senior lock-in, watching *Jaws* out by the pool. They were projecting it on the side of the gym, and you sat down next to me and acted weird for the next thirty minutes before starting a conversation. You must have pulled your deck chair an inch closer a dozen times. And then you asked me out once the kids were in the locker rooms changing into their pajamas. It was awkward and beautiful, and you don't remember at all."

"You're remembering it wrong," Dane said, trying to slide his hand into Muriel's tightly folded arms as she twisted away. "That was the third or fourth time we met. The first time was the test, the second was when you told me the students did so well on it, then there were two or three near misses when I tried to talk to you, but you were surrounded, and then it was the poolside movie night."

"None of that was me," Muriel hissed. "How many women on that faculty did you ask out?"

Dane scratched his head. "How many did I ask out?" he said, "Or how many said yes?"

"How could you not remember?"

"It was the test."

Muriel narrowed her eyes, and even in the moonlit attic, Dane could see the distrust in her eyes.

"You were working at one of the computer stations in the lounge," he started slowly, painting the scene for her. "You were annoyed at some of the male teachers causing a ruckus, watching the soccer game and having a shoving match on the couches behind you. You had told them to cut it out already, and I could tell you were getting super frustrated."

Muriel's posture softened, her arms uncrossed, but her hands stayed in her lap.

Dane nodded. "I walked over and asked what you were working on and if you needed any help. I told you the game would be done in about ten minutes, and the guys would move on. You were trying to connect the questions to the standards in the lesson plans, and the two programs wouldn't work together. You didn't even want to, but the new department head was trying to flex."

Dane snapped his fingers. "The guy with the head shaped like a triangle. You said he spent every meeting talking about everything except how to teach kids."

"Dr. Wolfe," Muriel said, leaning forward and resting her face in her left hand.

"Wolfe," Dane said, gently slapping her knee and shaking it. She brushed his hand off, but lightly.

"I told you our English department head had done the same thing, and it took at least eight meetings and twenty hours of YouTube videos to figure it out," Dane continued.

"You said it was too late to save your evaluation, but you could help me with mine."

Dane beamed and slid his hand around her shoulders, inching his crate a little closer to hers. "You remember now," he said. "Don't you?"

"That was you?"

Dane rotated his wrists in a showy gesture of presentation and bowed to Muriel. "'Twas I," he said. "And you didn't remember. How unromantic can you be?"

"I'm sorry," Muriel said, leaning towards him, the soft moonlight through the window making gold of her brown skin. "There were so many white men at that school, and the ones who weren't looking at me funny or acting like fools all the time were always trying to help me with something. Or both."

Dane shrugged and inched even closer to her.

Muriel smiled. "But you remembered." She kissed his cheek.

"Oh, it was a storybook romance for me," he said. "I helped you with your computer problem, probably sensed that you forgot all about me after, stalked you in the halls for the next three weeks waiting for the planets to align for me to talk to you, and then finally saw you alone at the movie. Then I made my move."

"Not much of a move."

"It worked, though. All according to plan."

He kissed her, and they stayed there for a few minutes holding each other. Soon, they tiptoed downstairs and made love as quietly as they could in Dane's boyhood bedroom before falling asleep.

That night, Dane dreamed about a girl standing under a streetlight, talking to a boy. His and Muriel's daughter. She had dark brown skin with hidden gold in it and curly hair like Muriel's, but she had Dane's height and jawline. She looked athletic like him, poise and grace in her posture, so strong and so beautiful. In his dream, he didn't know her name, but it didn't matter. He knew that he loved her.

9

JUST AFTER FIVE in the evening, Dane and Muriel sat across from each other at a restaurant near the house, the type of place that had eight different kinds of burgers on the menu and an extensive selection of both appetizers and kids meals. The place was a little too casual for Muriel, and the time way too early for Dane, but the rhythms of their moods had synced again and they each gave in a little. They both agreed that they had eaten out much more since moving in to help Branson than they had in months. Normally, they took turns cooking for six nights out of the week and went out for date night on Fridays. This arrangement helped them stay on budget and meet their savings goals, but it also required some compromise when it came to menu choices. Muriel cooked the Haitian dishes she had grown up with; *griot* and *soup joumou*. Dane, on his nights, mostly cooked healthy foods like fish and vegetables but had no patience for recipes with more than five ingredients.

When they moved into the old house they talked about keeping up their traditions, but both of them felt like interlopers in Branson's routines. They praised how efficiently Sabine took care of Branson and how easy she made it for them by preparing all his meals. They whispered about how sweet it was to get out more together, like when they were dating, but also about how much it put a dent in their budget.

What they didn't talk about, but Dane suspected they both knew, was how much they needed a buffer between spending the day preparing for the start of the school year—reading and lesson planning—and then taking care of Branson at night. They didn't talk about how every night they got the easier part of the job of caring for the old man or how they still dreaded the moment when Sabine walked out the door and left them in charge. Their responsibilities only involved making sure he bathed and got to bed and generally being ready for any of his needs through the night, yet it felt daunting.

By quarter to six, they walked in the door while Sabine was cleaning up after Branson's dinner and packing her things to leave. Dane was on bath duty; Muriel had already insisted she would not take turns on anything involving the bathroom. She said she still had too much respect for her father-in-law to see him in such a humiliating context. Even so, Branson generally took care of himself. Dane's part was mainly to make sure he actually bathed and to sit outside the door and listen in case the old man fell or called for help. He shuddered at the thought that one day he would have to open the bathroom door.

Bath duty usually took a while, not only because Branson moved much slower now, but also because he had always been one for long showers. Dane remembered several arguments between his parents about bathroom courtesy, specifically about saving a little hot water for the rest of the family. They weren't arguments the way other couples might argue; in fact, they mostly consisted of Dane's mother upbraiding his father for his selfishness and his father apologizing with downcast eyes and gritted teeth—and expression that was likely to turn into a grin any second. Dane remembered those moments well because it was the only time he had ever heard his mother use a curse word. It comforted him a little to know the old man still had some of these quirks, that some aspects of his personality were still holding on.

He wondered how long it would take for them to change.

Muriel generally used this time for herself. She would catch up on a novel or do some puzzles on her tablet. This night, however, Dane tiptoed out of his father's bedroom after bedtime to find her sitting at the top of the stairs, her back to the slightly opened attic door.

He smiled at Muriel, dreaming of the way their last trip to the attic had turned a burgeoning squabble into a night of furtive lovemaking. "You wanna go look again?"

Muriel crinkled her nose and grinned back sheepishly. Winking at him, she rose to her bare feet and padded through the gap in the door without touching it. Dane followed, his heartbeat quickening as he climbed the stairs.

Muriel knelt in front of the window, leaning her elbows on the frame, while Dane pulled up a crate beside her. His knees crackled as he settled onto it. Again, Branson and Gwen were down there together in the fading light of sunset under the street light that would turn on soon, holding hands in the awkward place where desire and naivete converge.

"It's their favorite spot," Muriel whispered, squeezing Dane's thigh.

Dane rubbed her back with the flat of his hand, and watched the young couple downstairs in their wordlessly intimate conversation.

Muriel sighed, arching her back into Dane's touch like a contented cat. "I love your parents. Loved the way they would cling to each other without . . ." she paused, closed her eyes, ". . . without demanding anything."

"I wonder how many memories they made under that streetlight," Dane said.

Shifting her weight from the edge of the window, Muriel draped her arms over Dane's legs, resting her head against his shoulder. Downstairs, Gwen and young Branson held hands, the tips of their fingers interlaced in awkward affection.

"They always had their hands on each other, right until the end," Muriel said. "Mom would put her hand on his shoulder when she walked by him or rub his leg when they sat together."

Dane nodded, slipping his arm around Muriel, pulling her close.

"Did you ever notice how she would pinch your father's cheeks and then kiss them?" she asked.

Dane pinched Muriel's waist. "You mean she used to love up on him," he said flatly, "Pop was never one for all the touchy-feely stuff."

"But he never got tired of it," Muriel corrected. "He always had that little mischievous grin when she touched him."

The couple downstairs sneaked a quick kiss in the lamplight, and Muriel giggled. She twisted in Dane's embrace, turning to look up at him. The light through the window made stars in her black eyes.

"You know," she whispered, "all that touchy-feely stuff between your mom and dad was what convinced me to marry you."

Dane dipped forward and kissed Muriel's waiting lips. "Then thank God for the touchy-feely stuff."

Muriel turned again to the window, mooning over the couple downstairs. "I wonder sometimes," she said, suddenly serious, "how different we would be together if we had met when we were young like that."

"Oh, no doubt, we never would have gotten together if you had known me back then," Dane said. "It took me at least twenty-five years to get this dope."

Muriel kissed his cheek, her eyes still focused on the window.

"Your parents had decades together," she mused. "There's something beautiful about growing up with someone before growing old with them. Sometimes I just wish we had more memories together."

As they watched the young couple downstairs, three more figures strolled into view down the sidewalk, backlit by flood of fiery orange and red light from the setting sun. Three young men. They walked towards the couple, each of them dressed in the same black leather jacket and dark blue jeans. Each of them wore a slightly different hairstyle, but all three were slicked back with so much grease that Dane thought he could smell it if he concentrated enough.

"I don't like this," Muriel hissed.

Dane's heart beat faster and his lower back suddenly ached as his muscles tensed into knots. Downstairs, Branson bristled as the boys approached with stupid smiles of cruelty on their faces. Gwen looked from the boys to Branson and pressed her hand to his chest, just over his heart. He focused back on her for a moment and seemed to relax.

The boys in the leather jackets drew closer. The smallest was about the same size as Branson, but the other two were bigger than Branson by a couple of inches and more than thirty pounds. The one walking out front, the biggest of the three, cupped his hands around his mouth and shouted something.

Branson push Gwen's hand away from his chest, but she grabbed his arm. The other two made kissing gestures at the couple as they drew closer still. Gwen whispered something into Branson's ear. He nodded and leaned back against the lamppost.

As they passed, the one out front looked Branson in the eye and slapped Gwen's behind, directly in the center, low enough to get the curve of her figure and hard enough to make her step forward from the force of the blow.

Dane winced and edged forward on the crate. He glanced at Muriel and she cringed, touching her fingertips to her mouth.

"*Gate san*," Muriel growled through gritted teeth. "Just like those boys when I was in high school."

Dane whipped his head sideways to look at her. Suddenly he also wished he had known Muriel back then.

But a movement from the street drew his attention back to the window. For a moment, it looked as if nothing would happen. The boys in the jackets kept walking, laughing and pushing each other as they went, and Gwen looked after them, her hands instinctively dropping to her backside to protect and cover herself. Muriel shook her head as if she understood the gesture completely.

But as soon as Gwen dropped her hands, the entire scene changed. The next few seconds were hard to follow, whether because of Dane's vantage point or the speed of the movements.

Freed from Gwen's calming hand, Branson covered the distance between himself and the boys in one step. The closest one to him, one of the taller ones, must have heard him coming, but too late. He turned around into Branson's right fist against the side of his jaw and crumpled to the sidewalk just outside the lamppost's circle of light.

Branson leaped over the unconscious boy with the same forward momentum and tackled the smallest of the three to the ground. The boy's head bounced off the concrete, and Branson used the dazed moment to straddle him. The third and biggest boy grabbed Branson's left arm, but Branson slipped free. The boy on the floor recovered a bit, threw his arms in front of him in an awkward defensive gesture, but Branson punched through it twice and then a third time. The boy turned his head and slapped at Branson's face in a panic, but every one of Branson's punches connected, and a quick, broad stream of blood ran from the boy's nose and one of his ears.

Branson reared back for another punch, but the biggest boy knocked him clean off his friend with a powerful kick to the ribs. The injured boy rolled over and started to crawl away while his bigger friend bent over Branson and grabbed a handful of his T-shirt. His fist crashed into Branson's eye socket twice, and then he paused.

Even from the attic, Dane could see why he stopped. Centered in the circle of light, Branson's face shone clearly, and he was smiling. The side of his face was already bright red and swelling, threatening to close his eye on the left side, but his mouth was twisted in a spiteful, venomous grin.

"Why is he smiling like that?" Muriel shrieked.

Before she could finish the thought, Branson kicked his attacker's knee, bending it dangerously sideways and dropping him to the ground. Instantly, Branson hopped to his feet and kicked the downed boy in the ribs, reared back, and kicked again. The boy curled up, giving Branson his back and covering his ribs with his arms.

Branson's entire body seemed rigid with rage. He was facing away from Dane and Muriel, and they could see the muscles in his back through his sweaty shirt. His hands curled into rock-hard fists, and he stepped towards the ball of a boy cowering under him.

Then Gwen stepped out from behind the streetlight. She laid a gentle hand on Branson's shoulder as he took another step towards the boy, and it was as if all the fury and electricity drained out of him at once. He turned around and looked into her face, his left eye starting to close from the swelling. She touched the puffy, raw flesh around his eye. He winced at first but then leaned into her touch.

The three boys limped away, two of them flanking the third and holding him up, but as far as Dane could tell, Branson and Gwen didn't notice them at all. Gwen leaned forward and kissed the swollen area, and his entire face turned the same bright shade of red, extending down his neck and stopping just above the ripped collar of his t-shirt. She said something to him, and while Branson looked away from her, at the light above, at the ground near his feet, her words clearly impacted him. He kissed her back, on the side of her cheek, touching the corner of her mouth.

The two of them walked down the sidewalk, beyond the lamppost's circle of light and in the direction the boys had come from. Dane and Muriel watched them until they disappeared into the darkness.

Muriel stayed on her knees in front of the window for a few seconds more. Dane watched her closely, shaking her head and blinking hard as if she had caught herself staring at the sun. She eased up and settled down onto a crate, with both hands on the sides to steady herself.

"Grandmé was right," she mumbled, "not all magic places are good." She looked up into Dane's face, fear widening her eyes and wrinkling her brow. "She would tell me, 'Go ahead little girl, if you can't hear, you will feel.'"

Dane pulled her into his arms, felt the tension in her shoulders and the tears starting to wet her face.

"I never should have come up here," she went on, "Grandmé would have locked that devil's door, and probably would have spat in front of it, too."

She wriggled free of Dane's grasp and crossed herself, kissing her fingers.

Dane reached for her, took her hands in his and bent his face to hers. "It's okay," he said, "It's in the past."

"Is it?" Muriel barked, "My God, why did he smile like that? And what did he do to those boys? Has that smile always been in him?"

"They had it coming, didn't they?" Dane said, "You saw what they did. They had it coming."

Muriel stood to her feet, her arms wrapped around her as if she were holding herself together, afraid she would fall apart into a heap.

"No," she said, not just her head, but her entire body shaking back and forth, "He wouldn't do that. Magic places lie sometimes, and your father wouldn't fight like that, smile like that."

Dane held her shoulders, steadied her, and looked into her eyes. "You don't know him like I do," he said.

Wiping her face with the heels of her hands, Muriel walked out of the attic and softly closed the door behind her.

His father's smile, so full of unhinged hurt and rage, the smile of a man who had grown so used to violence that it felt like home. Dane closed his eyes and tried to make the memory of that smile go away. Maybe Grandmé was right, and not all magic was good.

Still, he wanted to cherish one thing he had seen. The way Gwen's touch had drained all the rage and violence out of her man, even at his worst moment. The idea that one person could love someone so purely, kill the beast inside them and give them back themselves. Dane knew the weight of his father's fist and the power in his body, and the idea that a love so powerful and intense could stop even the most brutal anger with a touch gave him hope.

THE NEXT DAY was Friday, normally the high point of Dane's week, but this week Sabine had the weekend off. He and Muriel would have to care for Branson alone, all weekend. Sabine had arranged for them all to have dinner together, saying she needed to prepare them for some changes in Branson. She and Muriel cooked together, enjoying the company and reminiscing about "back home," while Dane slipped out to the gym, worked on some lesson plans, and generally worried the time away until Friday evening. By late afternoon, they all sat down together around the small table in the kitchen. Dane and Sabine next to Branson.

"I don't want to alarm you, either of you," Sabine whispered, after they had prayed over the meal and started eating, "but your father is getting worse in some ways."

Branson ate from a bowl half-filled with rice and red beans while the other three had plates with the rice, chicken, and salad. Dane watched Branson struggle to keep the rice on his spoon, something he had expected and even grown used to. Like a child learning to eat by himself, more of the rice ended up in his lap than in his mouth.

"Let me get that, Pop." Dane reached over to move the bowl closer, but

Sabine shook her head and subtly raised her open hand to signal him to back off.

"Let him do it," she said. "We can always clean up after."

Branson took another spoonful out of the bowl, careful to drag it along the edge of the inside to keep more on the spoon, but his hand tilted as he brought it toward his mouth, and all the rice spilled onto the table. He rapped the spoon on the table and muttered something Dane couldn't make out. He tried again. Half of the spoonful made it to his mouth, the rest fell to his chin and his lap.

Taking his napkin, Dane reached over to wipe his father's mouth, but Sabine made the same stopping motion with her palm, so he sat back and folded his arms. Muriel moved some of her rice around in her plate, looking straight into her food and tapping her foot under the table.

"You're doing fine, Mr. Schottmer," Sabine said between bites from her own plate. "Can I get you anything else? Do you want some chicken now?"

"I don't like this food," Branson said, pushing himself away from the table.

"We have some chicken," Sabine answered calmly, "and there's some salad. You can eat them with a fork. Do you want something to drink?"

"I want potatoes," Branson said, rapping the table again with his spoon. "I don't like this food. Gwen makes mashed potatoes the way I like them. I want her to make mashed potatoes." He looked across the table at Muriel, who looked back at him over her hands, covering her mouth and nose.

"I don't understand why Gwen can't make my food for me."

Muriel moved her hands over her eyes as her shoulders heaved. Dane bit his lip and looked pleadingly at Sabine as if she could stop this, but she just returned his stare and nodded. She reached over and rubbed the back of Branson's shoulder.

"Gwen is gone, Mr. Schottmer," she said softly. "She died almost two months ago, and she's buried with your family."

Branson stared at Sabine, cocked his head to one side, and then looked at Dane, but Dane looked through the kitchen window into the backyard. "Oh," the old man said, taking his napkin from the table and wiping the food from his chin. He looked back at Sabine and smiled weakly. "You sang at her funeral."

Sabine took Branson's hand in both of hers and leaned toward him, smiling. "We all did. It was very beautiful."

"Beautiful."

"Do you remember how she used to cook for you?" Sabine asked, rubbing the back of Branson's hand. "How she would kick me out of the kitchen sometimes because she wanted to bake something for you?"

Branson nodded and smiled. He pulled his hand away from Sabine and took up his spoon again.

Muriel stood up, her brow creased with lines and her eyes red. She squeaked, "Excuse me," then turned and walked down the hall and upstairs.

Dane looked down the hall after her and then stared at the spot on the wall left behind her as she disappeared up the stairs. He inhaled and exhaled at a slow, controlled pace until he felt more stable. He turned back to Sabine. She nodded and gestured with her head to follow his wife.

Dane found Muriel sitting on the bed in his old bedroom, head between her knees, shaking with sobs. He sat down next to her, put his arm around her, and rubbed her back. He started to say something but didn't trust his voice, so he just sat there, his hand moving up and down over her spine as she gradually calmed.

After a few minutes, she sat up and put her arms around his neck, burying her face in his shoulder.

"It's bad," Dane said quietly into her ear.

She pressed her forehead into his shoulder and nodded.

"He's a good man," Muriel said into Dane's chest. "He doesn't deserve this. I don't want to see him like this."

Dane breathed slowly and deeply through his nose and stroked the back of her head, looking up at the top of the doorway.

"I didn't know he was getting this bad," she said. "I didn't think it was this bad."

"Neither did I."

Muriel pulled her head away from Dane's chest and looked up at him, pulling his face with two hands to make him look back at her. "But how could we not know?"

Dane looked into her eyes, bit his lip, and slowly shook his head.

Muriel burst into fresh tears. "What am I going to do without you?" she pleaded.

Dane let his mouth drop open, shocked out of his train of thought.

"Baby," he said after staring at her for a moment, "you don't have to worry about that."

"I can't help it," she said through tears.

"Whenever you feel that way, just remember" — Dane cupped her face in his hands— "I am going to outlive all of you soda-drinkers and fast-food junkies."

Muriel pounded his chest with both her fists. "That's not funny!" she shouted, but her tears gave way to laughter.

Dane pulled her close and rocked with her at the edge of the bed. Sabine would be leaving soon, for the whole weekend, and he knew he had to get down there to take over. But Muriel was right. It was so bad. His father had wound down like an old watch when Dane wasn't looking, and Dane was having a hard time forgiving himself for letting it all creep up on him, for ignoring the way Branson had been forgetting things for years, losing more and more energy every day, mixing up his words and his thoughts.

He told himself he had been so focused on his mother and her health— they all had—and Branson just hadn't been a top priority for a while. But the more honest part of him told him it wasn't true. In reality, Sabine had been there to take care of all the ugly and difficult parts he didn't want to even think about.

Dane had paid some bills, managed some accounts, and more or less stayed away. And even though he didn't want to think about himself this way, maybe he just didn't care as much about his father as he did about his mother.

Something intangible and indescribable had come between Dane and his father, made it almost impossible for them to truly see each other. It had started small and had grown imperceptibly slowly, taking decades to become the high wall separating them. And now, apparently, Dane had only a short time left to break it down or get over it—if he could make the climb, if his father could understand any moves he would make. He didn't believe his father would even be able to comprehend Dane's forgiveness for his failures as a father. Even worse, he couldn't yet summon the will to forgive.

Even after forcing himself to get up and walk back downstairs, Dane puzzled over how he would get through the weekend. Sabine must have seen something in his eyes when he came into the living room, where she sat next to Branson, her purse in her lap, because she got up and hugged him.

"You can handle this," she said, her hand still on Dane's shoulder. "We can talk about the next steps next week."

She kissed his cheek, squeezed his upper arm, and then walked out the door, singing her goodbyes to Muriel over her shoulder.

Next steps. The last time he and Sabine spoke about next steps, it had been about his mother. How long ago? Six months, maybe eight. If time could slip away that fast, then he had to start chipping away at the wall between him and his father, even if he found nothing on the other side.

* * *

Dane intended to wake up before his father, partly to get his breakfast ready but partly to keep him under constant watch once he got up. He had hoped to wake his father up with breakfast already made, but when he passed the old man's bedroom, he found the door wide open and the room empty. Instinctively, Dane ran upstairs to the attic, touching the keys in his pocket, trying to remember if he had locked the door since he had been up there with Muriel.

The door opened wide. Dane burst through it to find his father sitting on the crate in front of the window, smiling, his hands over his mouth like a boy on Christmas morning waiting for the signal to unwrap presents. The old man turned and saw Dane. He put his finger to his lips before motioning him to come over. Dane leaned over, resting his hands on his knees until he caught his breath, and then sat next to his father on the other crate.

He recognized his father's old sky-blue Beetle coming down the street toward the old house, but he had never seen it look so new. The car seemed to move in slow motion. When it finally stopped in front of the house, his father fairly jumped out of the driver's side door and raced toward the house, keys in hand.

Dane looked on, worried at what could have possibly happened to make his father drive so slowly and then move so quickly. The younger version of Branson looked up, grinning. Dane saw his mother sitting in in the back seat on the passenger's side, looking more like the woman he remembered growing up than the teenager he'd seen kissing his father under the streetlamp. Although he could barely see her face from the angle of the attic window, she didn't seem worried at all. In fact, she seemed very relaxed, but Dane wondered why she would be sitting in the back seat with only the two of them in the car.

Young Branson came running back out of the house and across the yard, top speed, skidding to stop at the rear car door. He paused there with his hands on his knees, catching his breath.

Once young Branson seemed to catch his breath, he gingerly pulled the door handle and opened the door slowly, reaching inside with both hands. He pulled his wife out and onto her feet, with one hand supporting her lower back and the other under her left arm. Once she had gotten to her feet, his father had stepped back. Dane saw the baby in his mother's arms, wrapped in a sky-blue blanket, almost matching the color of the car behind her.

"We didn't even have a car seat back then," Branson said, resting his hand on Dane's leg and squeezing his thigh, while the Branson downstairs hovered around his wife holding the baby as they slowly crept into the house. "Gwen just sat in the back with you and held you to her chest over the seatbelt. It took us over an hour to decide how to get you both in the car, and where to sit, and how to hold you."

The old man leaned into the window so he could see at a more downward angle, and Dane found himself doing the same. The new father walked alongside the mother, holding his hands underneath her arm as she carried the newborn baby boy, ready to catch him if she should trip, but also keeping a safe distance.

"I didn't know what to do with you," Branson said through the biggest smile Dane had ever seen on his father's face. "You were so little and so alive and important, and I just knew I was going to break you."

Dane laughed at the idea of his father, always so athletic and agile, worried about holding a baby. He had seen the man play full-contact football with the men in the family at barbeques, seen him handle a basketball at fifty better than some of the kids on his high school basketball team.

Even now, with Alzheimer's causing his hands to shake, his father still walked with such an easy grace that Dane sometimes forgot how much ground the old man had lost. Branson tore his eyes from the window for a second at hearing Dane's laughter and put his hand firmly on the back of his son's neck.

Dane flinched at the bony fingers gripping him and pulled back, remembering the last time he had laughed at his father and the way Branson had exploded in anger. But then the old man pulled his head close with an unimaginably strong arm and kissed his son on the cheek before looking back through the window to watch the family of three downstairs enter the house, with as much wonderment in his eyes as if he were watching the holy family leave the stable.

"We waited until I was almost forty to have a child because I just knew I would be a terrible father," Branson said, staring through the window at the empty car on the curb. "What did I know about babies? About kids?" He put his hands on the window and flattened them into the curved glass. "We almost waited too late. Your mom was getting older, too, and we had already lost two babies before you."

As close as he had been with his mother and as many years as they had shared, Dane had never known about any other babies besides himself. He looked up at the top of the window, opening his eyes wide to try to get control.

"I think that was my fault too," Branson said. "I wasn't sure I ever wanted to have babies. People thought there was something wrong with us back then. Everybody got married and had babies. It was just what was expected of you. If they found out we were on the pill, they really would have thought something was wrong with us. And then, when I finally gave in and wanted to . . ."

His voice broke as if he were choking.

Dane watched his father struggle. Branson looked through the window and held on to Dane's neck as if he thought his son would get away from him. Dane tensed his neck and shoulders under the old man's grip but didn't fight to get free nor try to move any closer. A couple of tears flowed from his father's face now, and every impulse in Dane told him to put his arm around the old man, tell him things hadn't turned out so badly, tell him he had been a decent father after all.

But he didn't.

Instead, he sat there under the firm grip of his aged father's hand and stared out the window at the past. The grip which had tenderly carried his tiny baby into the house; his first born, or rather, his only born of at least three. The same firm hand had snatched him up off the floor out of the midst of his toys so many times when he was a child, for some disobedience or another. The same hand had once almost twisted his ear clean off while he demanded that Dane apologize to his mother for some sarcastic remark. Now that firm hand held on to Dane's shoulder tightly, in desperation, but Dane just couldn't bring himself to reach back.

Dane cursed himself for not moving closer, for not closing the gap. *Just move closer*, Dane thought. *Hug him, touch him, say something. Pick up a hammer and swing it at the wall.* In his head, he called himself a baby and a loser, the way he had done when he had to work up the nerve to ask a girl out or walk onto the basketball court in a close game. But no amount of cursing or cajoling could get his hand to move.

After a few minutes of silence, Branson released his son, stroked the back of his head, and walked out of the room.

Dane had lost championships, had lost jobs and girlfriends, but nothing in his past came close to the self-loathing sense of failure which overwhelmed him as his father disappeared down those stairs.

11

DANE DIDN'T SPEAK much for the rest of the day, and, as usual, Muriel left him alone to figure things out, only casting him an open look from time to time. Dane had seen that look so many times; the eyebrows up, the slight smile, and the cocked, curious head. She had worn it for days at a time in the past, and Dane knew the message it sent: *I'm here if you want to talk, but I'm not chasing you down.*

He tried several times during the day to broach the subject with her. The first time, he had caught her alone in the kitchen, but waited so long to work up the nerve that his father started calling for his breakfast. Later, as they sat together on the couch surrounded by their schoolwork, Dane noticed a lull in the workflow and struck up a conversation with Muriel about Branson. They talked routines and meal planning, but Dane failed to steer the conversation towards the swarms of disparate emotions swirling and merging in his head. Part of him want to be honest with her, but every little task and routine provided a hiding place for a man who wasn't completely willing to step into the light.

By the time night fell, Dane's back ached and his shoulders felt as if they were stone. Besides the work of caring for a grown man in much the same way one would care for a child, he had forced on himself the weight of emotional work without finding a convenient place to lay it down. In addition, since he had been staying in his father's house, his schedule and his internal clock had started to adjust and reset. He felt hungry by four, sleepy by seven, and annoyingly wide awake early in the morning during summer vacation, when no work called him out of bed.

Once he lay down in his old bedroom, bathed and comfortable on the outside but riled up on the inside, Muriel caressed his chest and arms in that gentle, evocative way she had when he held back his words, as if this small, repetitive motion could get them to flow.

Dane slipped his arm under her shoulders as she settled into his embrace. The bed, so much smaller than their own, felt as if they were trying to sleep together on a couch. It had its benefits, Dane thought, but sleep and comfort weren't on the list.

"It was a good day for Pop," she said, "no trouble at all. Sabine would be proud of us."

Dane screwed up his face as if to gently disagree.

"No?" Muriel asked. "Did I miss something? What happened?"

Dame heard an urgency in her voice, a concern for the old man as bold and vocal as her concern for her husband was muted and meditative.

Dane pulled her in closer and fondled her ear. "What if we had a kid?" he asked.

Muriel pulled away from him, sat up onto her elbow, and looked him in the face.

"A kid?" she asked, loudly at first and then more softly but forcefully. "Like, a human child?"

Dane nodded and smiled. "I know," he said, chuckling at her wide eyes and worried brow. "I know, but don't you ever think about it?"

Muriel pressed the palm of her hand to Dane's forehead, held it there for a moment, moved it to the side of his neck, and then shook her head. "My love, I am forty years old and a Black woman. Do you know that just those two things put me in the high-risk category for pregnancy?" She turned his face from side to side, roughly, looking into his eyes, while he laughed at her.

"So you never think about it?" he said.

"I thought about it," Muriel responded, sitting up fully and putting a pillow in her lap between them. "When I was twenty-five and single. I thought about it when I was thirty and single, and we hadn't met yet, and my mother started setting me up with every older single man in her church. I even thought about freezing my eggs before I saw how much it cost." She leaned over him and whispered, "I don't think I ever told you, but at one time, when I was about thirty-three, a year before we met, I gave some serious thought to just going out and getting pregnant."

"No," Dane said. "You?"

"*Wi, mwen,*" she said, "and one of my girlfriends talked me off the ledge."

Dane sat up, adjusting himself in the bed to avoid knocking Muriel out of it completely. "Inaya?"

"*Egzakteman,* young man. Take a prize from the treasure box." She squeezed her hips next to him, both of them sitting up against the flat headboard. "Inaya is a single mom with a seven-year-old girl and a baby daddy to raise. She makes it look easy, but she told me three or four stories that were some of the best therapy I've ever gotten. Cured me" —Muriel snapped her fingers loud enough to reverberate in the bedroom— "like that."

"So not even a little since then?" Dane asked.

Muriel pushed her toes out from under the covers and watched herself wiggling them. After a pause, she looked back at Dane and grasped his chin in her hand to make him look back at her. "Did something happen?"

Dane pulled his face out of Muriel's grip but kept his focus on her round brown eyes. "I saw something upstairs," he said, "through the window."

"*Non, mesye,*" Muriel said, folding her arms and leaning back into the headboard. "Don't even tell me. I'm not messing with that ever again."

"But it was nice, wasn't it?"

"Yes, nice," she said, with a touch of sarcasm in her tone, "but it won't always be nice. Sometimes, to win us to our harm, the instruments of darkness tell us truths, to betray us."

Dane sat straight up in bed, almost knocking her over. "Macbeth?" he blurted, checking his volume after. "Impressive."

Muriel shrugged and brushed some imaginary dirt off the shoulder of her pajamas.

"Still, using Shakespeare against me is a little low, don't you think?"

"And this thing has got you talking about babies?" She pulled her feet back under the covers and turned to face him. "Even if it were possible, which it's not, because I'm too old and I don't want to, we talked about this. We had a plan. Didn't we say we wanted to be able to travel whenever we wanted? That we wanted to save money so we could retire without having to teach when we're seventy?"

Dane patted the scarf covering Muriel's hair and smoothed out a wrinkle before she swatted his hand away.

"But do we really travel that much?" he asked.

"Then let's travel," Muriel answered immediately. "We have money saved, a lot of money for a couple of teachers."

"That's true," Dane said. Watching Muriel's unchanging face, he added, "You're right. You're totally right." He took her hand in his and kissed it, and she softened and settled back against him.

He kissed her forehead in the lines of light through the blinds, and she kissed him back on his cheek.

"So, you never think about it?" he asked softly.

She kissed him again on the cheek and then closer to his lips, right at the edge of his mouth, and he knew she was ending the conversation. He kissed her back. "Never?"

"Maybe, sometimes," she said and slid her arms around him, kissing him where his neck curved into his shoulder.

They kissed for a few minutes, pulling the covers over themselves. "Can you take off the headscarf?" Dane asked, scratching Muriel's back under her T-shirt.

She stroked his face and looked into his eyes. "Is it going to be worth putting it back on again?"

Whispering into her ear so closely that his lips brushed her earlobes, Dane said, "I will live in thy heart, die in thy lap, and be buried in thy eyes."

Muriel smiled and shook her head as she untied the scarf and laid it on the nightstand behind her. "Can I ask you something, my love?"

"Anything."

"Did you ever sneak a girl in here when you were growing up?"

"No, baby," Dane said. "You're so special to me."

Muriel smiled and bit him softly on his earlobe.

"Now," Dane continued, "I can't promise that my father never did."

"*Bon nwi*," Muriel said and rolled over, her back to Dane in the tiny bed, her hand reaching for her head covering. Dane laughed and put his arms around her, kissing the back of her neck until she put back the scarf.

MORE THAN A week passed before Dane had time to visit the attic again. His father needed more and more help by the day, or at least it seemed so to Dane. Between tying shoes, helping with meals, and otherwise supervising just about everything Branson did, the evenings were filled with endless activity for both Dane and Muriel until the old man went off to bed around eight. Then they kept the house quiet for a couple of hours before slipping up to bed themselves, sleeping like soldiers in the field, with ears open for any movement or noise. To Dane, it felt like all the duties of parenting a toddler but with all the awkwardness of performing them for a grown man.

On weekdays, with Sabine in the house, Dane and Muriel filled the day with reading and lesson planning for the start of school, only a month away. Sabine kept Branson out of the way as the two teachers sat on the couch together, laptops in front of them on matching wooden caddies filled with their pens and sticky notes on one side and a couple of slim books on the other. A short wall of textbooks on the couch separated them, English readers on Dane's side and history books on Muriel's. She sipped steaming coffee, and he guzzled iced green tea, and together they avoided talking about what would happen when they both had to start back at work full-time again.

Branson's walks with Sabine grew longer and longer. Sometimes Branson would come back from his walk with a triumphant smile. They all called those good days. But more often came back flushed and sweating, and he wanted to lay down for a nap immediately. Sabine had to cajole him into washing his face and eating a little something first. Sometimes Muriel accompanied them for some fresh air and girl talk, but less frequently as the first day of school drew nearer.

"We're back," Muriel sang to Dane one afternoon as she dropped into his lap on the couch, playfully interrupting his work. Branson plodded into the kitchen behind Sabine.

"How did it go?" Dane asked, one arm around Muriel's waist while his other hand scrolled through a document on his laptop.

Muriel's face straightened, the cheer draining from her cheeks. She bit her lip and squinted her eyes. "We barely made it around the block," she said, whispering to Dane, with one eye watching the kitchen doorway.

Dane pushed the laptop aside. "You were gone for an hour," he said, confused.

Muriel tapped his lips with her fingertips and shifted into the couch beside him. "It's taking him longer and longer every day," she said. "It's different."

Puzzled, Dane searched her eyes.

"No more jogging, not even a few steps like before, no showing off, walking backwards," she said, resting her hand on the back of Dane's neck and twirling her finger in his short hair. "He barely waves at the ladies anymore."

"Oh, no," Dane said, clapping his hand over his mouth and feigning alarm, "It's worse than we could have imagined."

Muriel shot him a reproachful look that straightened his smirk. "Not funny," she said. "You're not out there to see him. Before he even gets to the first corner," she paused, hunched her shoulders and imitated the old man's heavy breathing.

Dane looked over his shoulder into the kitchen where his father was listlessly eating a sandwich, his head dipping like a toddler falling asleep before naptime.

"I don't think I want to see that," he said.

"Maybe you should," Muriel said, taking his hand and interlacing her fingers with his. "It reminds me of when Grandmé died back home. I was little, maybe five or six, and I used to hate walking to the store with her. She was so slow, and it took so long. I would run ahead of her and let her catch up the entire way or rush her through the store. I should have spent that time talking to her, listening to her. She died a year later."

Dane kissed her temple and pulled her close, "You were just a child," he said.

Muriel kissed him back. "Yes, maybe," she said, "but those are the only memories I have of my *grann*. Child or not, I should have done better."

Dane thought about the days slipping by. Muriel may have been a child when her grandmother passed, but Dane wasn't.

"If only I'd had someone to tell me to do the right thing," Muriel sighed, wrapping her arm around him and patting his shoulder. "If only someone wiser than me, more beautiful and compassionate, had shown me the error of my ways and set me on the right path. If only someone with dark, alluring eyes and a body like a goddess had been bold enough to . . ."

Dane interrupted her by pushing her over on the couch and she giggled as he held her down.

"Fine," he said, "I'll go for a walk with him tomorrow."

The next day Dane kept his word and switched places with Muriel. It turned out to be a "good day," as if having Dane along invigorated the old man. Still, when they got back, Branson once again plodded to the kitchen like a toy robot winding down.

Dane kissed Muriel as he passed her on the couch working. He sneaked past Branson's open bedroom door and up the stairs to the attic window. Although he intended to make sure he had locked the door, he slipped inside the attic room instead and sat down on the crate in front of the window, almost before he knew he had done it, like a smoker with their fingers unconsciously at their lips. He felt a vague desire, a compulsion to see more.

At first, it looked as if he had come up there for nothing. Nothing happened through the window for several minutes. Thinking Muriel might call out or come checking on him any second, or that Sabine and Branson might get home, Dane started to get up to leave, in the same distracted way he would leave a basketball game he didn't really want to tear himself away from. He kept his eyes on the window as he slowly rose from his makeshift seat but dropped back down when he saw a familiar movement on the street below.

The same old sky blue Beetle slowly glided down the road, carefully pulling up to the curb outside the house. The little car had a couple more scratches on it and a new dent on the rear fender facing him, but otherwise, it looked exactly the same as the last time he had seen it through the window. It came to a slow, gentle stop in front of the house, just like it did before. However, this time, he could see his mother sitting in the front seat instead of the back. She was still young and beautiful, but she looked tired, like she could fall asleep any second. He could barely see his father in the driver's seat from the high angle.

Neither one of them got out of the car.

Dane watched as a couple of minutes went by, neither of them moving nor speaking. Minutes went by, and then a little boy walked onto the front lawn from the house. The boy held hands with a woman Dane didn't recognize, someone who looked like she was in her fifties. The boy seemed about two years old and wore a red Sesame Street t-shirt Dane recognized from several old pictures of himself.

When the couple in the blue Beetle saw little Dane there on the grass, they looked at each other, held each other's gaze for a moment. Branson stepped out of the car and walked around to open the door for his wife. She sat there staring straight ahead down the street. After opening her door, he squatted on the curb next to her.

Dane watched his mother burst into a sob so sudden and deep it jerked tears from his own eyes before he could catch himself. She crumpled forward in the car and buried her face in her hands against the dashboard.

The toddler must have had the same reaction down in the grass because he screamed and tried to pull away from the woman, who in turn planted her feet, gripped his little hand more tightly, and held him back. When he kept wriggling and straining against her, she snatched him up into her arms, where he still struggled against her, pushing against her face and chest.

Young Branson still squatted by the car. He buried his face in his wife's shoulder and slid his arm over her legs. She nodded and patted him on the back, gently pushing him back as she swung her legs out of the car. As she stood up and Branson moved alongside her, his arm around her waist, Dane could see her rounded belly pushing forward against her yellow peasant dress. The dress had a high waist which rested on top of her abdomen. They took slow steps up the walkway towards the toddler squirming in the woman's arms. Dane couldn't take his eyes off the way his mother cradled her belly. Her hands never left her midsection until she reached out for the boy and took him into her arms. In an instant, the toddler calmed down and laid his head against his mother's chest.

The father downstairs stood behind his wife and child, and even from the attic, Dane could see the gleam of tears on the man's face. Young Branson mashed both hands into his eyes, and the woman who had been holding his son turned towards the house, away from the spectacle. After a beat, they walked towards the house together and disappeared under the porch awning.

Just then, Dane heard a door slam shut.

He jumped to his feet and looked guiltily over his shoulder as he desperately wiped his face with his shirt sleeve, but only saw the attic door, shut tight. For a moment, confusion washed over him until he realized it was just his father, closing the bathroom door or his bedroom door after lunch.

Muriel would be looking for him now, for sure, but he couldn't move to the door. He tried to refocus his thoughts, to pull himself together, but there were so many questions running through his head. Why hadn't his mother ever told him about this? His father had always been like a stone vault, but his mother? How would his life have been different with a little brother or sister? How did his parents deal with the pain?

Deep throbs of sadness pulsed through him, for both his mother and his father. He had never felt so connected to the old man, but even so, he couldn't help thinking about himself. Maybe his parents had spared him the heartbreak of losing a brother or sister, or maybe he had been too little to understand or feel it anyway, but he could feel a different kind of loss now and an insight into his father's pain he wouldn't have thought possible. Can you grieve somebody who doesn't exist? Is there another kind of heartbreak in losing the child you're not expecting?

Dane turned his back on the window and walked to the attic door. He could hear the commotion of the women talking and preparing lunch, but it took him several minutes to fix his face and go downstairs to join them.

DANE CAME DOWN the attic stairs calling for Muriel. Peeking into his father's bedroom, he saw the old man sitting on the edge of his bed, both hands on his knees, in the exhausted and frustrated way he used to have after coaching a losing basketball game more than thirty years ago. As a boy, Dane had learned to tread cautiously when his father's normally proud, agile posture hunched and closed in on itself.

"You good, Pop?" he called through the doorway. Dane lingered for a minute, leaning against the open door frame and waiting for his father to respond.

Instead of looking up, Branson just waved him off with his left hand and then seemed to wince at the motion. "Fine," he growled.

"Okay," Dane nodded, turning to leave. Before he got to the top step down to the first floor, he returned to Branson's bedroom. "You want me to bring your lunch up here?"

"I'm coming," Branson snapped, but quietly, out of breath, and his voice trailed off at the end. He looked up at Dane, smiled faintly, and hoisted himself to his feet, pushing against his own knees with both hands.

Dane felt awkward. It was like watching the old man undress, seeing him almost naked. He turned to go but glanced over his shoulder one more time before turning the corner and descending the stairs. Still, something nagged at him, something about the way his father almost dragged himself to his feet. Even as his health had declined, there was still an easy grace about his walk and his movements. Sometimes it made Dane jealous in an irrational way. With all Branson's problems, with the Alzheimer's ravaging his nervous system, the old man still moved so well. In a rare moment of openness, Dane once admitted to Muriel how much he hoped he would have his father's same grace when he got that old.

He stopped at the bottom of the stairs, a feeling of dread growing in him and no way to know what it portended, except that something was wrong with his father. He turned and saw Branson reaching the top step. The old man paused at the top step. Too long, Dane thought. Grabbing the rail with his right hand, Branson braced his weight against it. Instead of bounding down the steps like he had when he was younger or shuffling down with the side to side movement he had acquired during the last few years, Branson turned sideways and leaned against the railing. He stepped down gingerly, feeling for the stair with his toes. Dane winced at the tentative and unnatural movement. Branson brought his left foot down carefully, paused, and then repeated the same careful sideways step.

Dane saw it in his head before it happened. His father's toes felt the edge of the next step and then staggered. He missed it by a couple of inches, and his foot struck the edge of the next step in the middle, sliding completely out from under him. Dane had the perfect vantage point to see it happen but the worst position from which to do anything about it.

Dane had heard about accidents like this seeming to happen in slow motion, but this happened so fast, as if Dane had blinked and the entire world changed. Before he knew it, his father was suspended in the air and then falling quickly, like a man tumbling into a pool or into bed after a hard day, but with an expression of complete terror.

Dane had no way to catch his father or stop his fall. At Branson's height, he just about cleared the entire length of the stairs. He didn't even stretch out his hands to stop himself.

Like a flashing light on the dashboard of the car, Dane focused on the only coherent thought in his frantic mind: *don't let Pop's head hit the floor.* Before he even knew it, his hands had extended, cradling the old man's head in the air before his body touched the steps, like catching a ball in midair with pure muscle memory. The old man's weight surprised Dane, knocked him to his knees, but Dane managed to cushion his father's head and neck as they hit the wooden. Dane's shin struck the bottom stair hard enough to make him see stars, but he made sure his hands remained underneath Branson's head. Upon impact, a jolt of pain stabbed his fingers and shot up his arms.

The rest of Branson's body struck the steps with a dull thud and a *snap* as his right arm landed hard between two stairs.

Dane looked into his father's eyes as they squeezed tightly closed and then relaxed. The old man's body went limp all over. His arm was bent in a slight but sickening crescent between the elbow and wrist.

"Sabine," Dane shouted, still cradling his father's head, afraid to move in case he would slip down the stairs. "Muriel! Sabine!" He shouted over and over until they came running around the corner.

"Call 911," Sabine barked at Muriel, without even looking in her direction.

She dropped to her haunches next to Dane. "Don't move, Dane," she commanded, gently turning over Branson's free arm and pressing her fingers to his wrist. "Keep him in exactly the same position."

Dane nodded, his eyes fixed on his father's other arm, twisted and pinned underneath his body. "Shouldn't we just ..."

"Don't talk," Sabine ordered him. Dane stiffened and held his father still.

While Muriel gave bursts of information through the phone between gasps of repressed sobs, Sabine ran to the living room and returned with every cushion and pillow she could carry. After placing them strategically around Branson's neck and back, she eased some of the weight in Dane's weary hands, then continued to probe different parts of the old man's body.

The ambulance arrived within fifteen minutes, the longest quarter of an hour Dane could have imagined. Sabine rattled off some numbers to the EMTs—pulse and other measurements— but Dane couldn't follow the conversation. He barely understood what Sabine was doing to his father while they held him and waited. Dane crouched stock still, his forearms burning, with his father's head in the palms of his hands until one of the EMTs touched his shoulder and soothingly asked him if he could take over. He shifted the weight of Branson's head into the paramedic's hands with slow precision and then rose to his feet. His legs were asleep, so he held on to the wall as he backed away, knives of pain stabbing his feet as the blood rushed back into them.

It seemed like the paramedics moved too slowly and took too many steps when he desperately wanted them to load his father into the ambulance and get him to the hospital, to safety. They eased Branson to the floor at the bottom of the steps, and the old man started to rouse a little. While they attached an oximeter to his finger, they asked him a few questions about his surroundings and what had happened. Apparently, they didn't like what they saw because within a minute of examining him, they dragged in a gurney and loaded Branson onto it.

The next minute, Dane, Muriel, and Sabine were left standing on the lawn watching the ambulance speed away with its lights flashing.

Dane drove to the hospital with Muriel, and Sabine followed behind. He could barely focus on the road. He kept seeing his father struggling at the top of those stairs, missing the step, and crashing down in front of him. Should he have moved quicker? Stayed up near his father longer? Helped him down the stairs? Muriel sat next to him, rubbing his shoulder, but it felt as if she were miles away.

Branson's arm had to be broken. Dane had heard the snap, could still hear it. He could still see the angle of the old man's arm as he lay there, slightly crooked, enough to set his teeth on edge when he pictured it. Whatever happened now, his father would need even more help from Dane, more constant attention. Every day he slipped farther away, and every time Dane looked at his father, another piece of the old man had vanished. First, the powerful and intimidating personality which had kept them so distant, then the agile and strategic mind, so crucial to Branson in the banks and on the basketball courts. Now the old man's body was betraying him, taking away all the athleticism and grace that had been the one thing they had in common, one of the only things about his father Dane had always respected and admired.

Dane wondered what would be left of his father when they got to the hospital. He also wondered whether his own mind and body would betray him in the same way one day. He wondered who would catch him when he fell.

Once both he and Sabine had parked their cars at the hospital and gone through the tedious checks required to find Branson, nurses shuffled Dane and Muriel into a small lounge. Sabine messaged them that she would be heading home after she exchanged information with the nursing staff. Every minute they waited there made them more suspicious that Branson was in a lot more trouble than they had originally thought.

After a while, a young doctor came in and introduced himself. "The arm is definitely broken, but that's not what you should be worried about," he said, easing into the chair across from Dane and leaning forward. "The paramedics ran an EKG on your father on the way over. It looks as if a heart attack preceded the fall, probably even causing it."

Muriel cried. Dane bit his lip and looked away from her as well as the doctor. He felt for his wife's hand and gripped it.

"Is he okay?" Dane asked.

The doctor nodded. "It sounds crazy, but the fall was a lucky accident. It was a mild heart attack according to the EKG results, but it could have been much worse without immediate attention. If he had just felt bad and decided to lay down, we would be having a different conversation."

"Worse?" Muriel whimpered.

"An untreated heart attack, one that continues to block blood flow to the heart, could be a lot worse than a broken arm."

Muriel leaned into Dane, and he pulled her close.

The doctor stood up. "Branson's already on blood thinners to help him recover from the heart attack and pain relievers for the arm and general pain," he said. "We're going to keep him overnight to monitor his heart and make sure the broken bone doesn't react negatively to the blood thinners. He's sleeping now, but you're welcome to go see him if you like."

He asked if Dane and Muriel had any questions before he left, and even though they said they didn't, they each had a million questions and concerns they couldn't put into words and didn't think he could answer.

When they walked into Branson's hospital room, they found him laying on his back in a deep, drug-induced sleep, even though Dane knew his father always slept on his side. His mouth gaped open, and loud, guttural snores filled the room. His broken right arm hung in a sling above his chest. A blinking oximeter pinched his finger. Electrodes clung to his chest with wires running to a display by the bed. Dane and Muriel squeezed together in the armchair next to the bed and watched the heartbeat displayed on the screen. A lifetime of fear lurked between every one of those green spikes.

Branson looked old. Not the spry and dashing "old" of a man with a full head of gray hair and a slight hitch in the step, but the frail and grotesque "old" of thin limbs and loose skin that shredded a man's dignity.

Muriel had stopped crying, and Dane had never started, but they both looked from the softly beeping display to the sleeping face with the same furrowed expression of concern. Dane pulled over another chair so they could sit more comfortably, telling Muriel it could be a long while before Branson woke. They pushed their chairs together. Muriel leaned on Dane's shoulder, exhaled, and fell asleep. Dane held vigil for a while longer. He watched for any movement, any change in the display. He greeted the nurses who tiptoed in from time to time with a weak smile and a nod. Mostly, he tried to will his father to get better, tried to pray, tried to send him his own strength if it were possible, and hoped they would be able to get him home soon. Near midnight, he shifted his weight closer to his wife in those awkward chairs, rested his head in her curls, and fell into a dreamless sleep.

Hours later, Dane snapped awake, shocked out of his sleep by a muffled scream. He lurched forward in his chair, scuttling it against the wall where it sounded with a wooden thunk. Rigidly upright in her chair, Muriel had her hands clapped over her mouth, exhaling labored breaths into her palms.

He glanced quickly at his father whose chest rose and fell softly, at the machines quietly tracking his vitals. He turned back to Muriel and rubbed her arm. "You good, Babe?" he asked, twisting his neck to relieve the kinks caused by his awkward sleeping position.

Muriel looked around the room, pressed her hand against the wall behind her, the arm of her chair, and Dane's arm. She pressed her hand to her lips, and pinched her cheeks together to feel them out, thrust a finger into her mouth, and dragged it across the bottom row of teeth.

"Bad dream?" Dane asked.

Muriel nodded. "Something about my grandfather."

Once she had calmed down, she told him that she had dreamed she was back in Haiti, in her family's house in Port-Au-Prince. "My room was just the same as before we left, back in 1980. All my dolls and pictures were there, even the same flowered sheets and stuffed dog," she said, her breath coming slower and more evenly as she spoke, "but somehow I was grown, and the bed was too small for me. My feet stuck out, off the end of the bed."

Dane pulled his chair back into its place next to her and sat, his eyes on the heart monitor beeping next to his father's bed. He stroked her back between her shoulder blades.

"I heard someone choking, so I walked down the hall, and the closer I got, the louder the coughing was, so I started running instead, down the steps to see what it was. At the bottom of the steps, I saw my grandfather," she said, looking at Branson's sleeping face, his slack jaw. "He looked just like he was before he died, before we moved to America. He was all doubled over, just tensed up and heaving with the coughing. He was holding on to his face like it was going come off if he let go."

Dane pulled her closer to him, under his arm, as close as the chairs would allow.

"I touched his back," she went on, "and his coughing stopped. He smiled at me, like he was so relieved, and his mouth was all gums. All his teeth were gone."

"'*Mesi, Petit Petit*,' Granpè said. He looked so tired and sick. His eyes were just like before he died, all cloudy and light brown, most of the color gone from them. But somehow, they were also childish, like a little boy's eyes.

"'You can't leave me behind, *pitit mwen*,' he said, and he touched my hand." Muriel gripped Dane's hand, and tears filled her eyes. "I didn't want to leave you, Granpè, I told him. You died. There was nothing else holding us here.

"But he just said, 'You can't leave me behind, Cheri.'"

Muriel sobbed, and immediately covered her mouth, sealing it with her palm, as her tears trickled down her fingers. Dane stroked her hair until she spoke again.

"I told him, I keep you in my heart, Granpè," Muriel said, trembling. "Just like I promised.

"Then he smiled at me again with that crooked toothless smile. He reached up to my face and cupped my cheeks in both of his hands. 'You can never leave me behind, *Pitit*.' he said.

"Then a pain shot through my mouth, between Grandpè's hands. It was like the worst toothache I ever had, but all over my mouth, in every tooth. I pulled away from him, and put my finger in my mouth, to see where the pain was coming from, and one of my molars felt soft, and sort of wiggled." Muriel stroked the sides of her jaw, ran her tongue over her bottom row of teeth. "I poked at it, and it just came right out in my hand. There was no blood, nothing wrong with it, but it just fell out, and the pain was still terrible. I felt something loose in my mouth and I spit it into my palm. It was a front tooth this time, and then another and another until my hands were full of white teeth."

She blew out a long sigh through pursed lips. "Then I woke up," she said, "and you were here."

Dane reached around her shoulders with both arms and held her tight enough to make her hold her breath for a moment. She leaned into the crook of his neck and smelled his skin, her chin resting on his shoulder.

"Dane," Muriel whispered, tapping his leg, "He's moving."

Branson shifted his weight slightly, almost imperceptibly, from one shoulder to the other, straining weakly against the sling suspending his arm over his chest. His eyes opened slowly and fell closed again twice before he seemed to keep them open enough to look around the room.

Dane hopped to his feet, landing on wobbly legs that burned with the restoration of blood flow after sleeping away the last three or four hours in those square-edged chairs with flat thin pads on the back and seat. Muriel sidled beside him, and they hovered over the old man. Dane rested his hand near Branson's head and leaned over his face to catch his attention while Muriel took his left hand and stroked the soft, thin skin on the back of it.

"Pop," Dane said softly, "Can you hear me?"

Branson cleared his throat, a long guttural sound that wasn't quite a cough but sounded as though it came from deep in his chest. "Where's Gwen?" he said, yawning and slurring his words. "Is Gwen all right?"

Dane looked sideways at Muriel, who rounded her eyes and bit her bottom lip.

"She's not here right now, Pop," Dane said. "You're in the hospital. How are you feeling?"

Branson struggled feebly against the cloth sling immobilizing his right arm. "My arm is stuck." Muriel gently laid Branson's hand by his side and pressed the call button for the nurse.

"You fell, Pop," Dane said. "You had a heart attack and fell down the stairs. You broke your arm."

The old man pulled at his sling once again, harder this time, and grunted. He settled back into his pillow and breathed out slowly through pursed lips. "It hurts."

Dane nodded and rested his hand gently on his father's left shoulder. "The nurse is coming with some more pain medicine."

Just inches away from his father's face, Dane tried to read every line, every movement, for some sign of health or improvement. Branson looked up at him, Dane imagined, the way a child would look at his father instead of the other way around, a blend of trust and fear.

Then Branson's eyes widened. Instead of lolling around half-lidded, they gazed right into Dane's own eyes, with a sense of clarity he hadn't seen in the old man for months. With a look of almost surprise, Branson reached up to grab Dane's forearm in a weak grip.

"You caught me," he whispered, and his head fell back to the mattress with a thud. "When I fell, you caught me."

Muriel whimpered slightly and slid her hand over Dane's shoulders, bending her body to fill the negative space his posture created. She breathed heavily through her nose and grabbed his shirt by the back, tight enough to pull his collar up uncomfortably against his neck.

Dane floated his hand across the top of his father's buzz cut and rested it gently on the crown of his head.

"Yeah, Pop," he said, with a rasping hitch in his voice, "I caught you. You remember?"

Branson nodded, half smiling and half wincing, and rested his head back into the pillow. Within a moment, his eyes were searching the room again, and his face darkened. "I'm so tired," he said.

Dane nodded and stroked his father's hair.

"You go to sleep, Dad," Muriel cooed, rubbing her husband's back. "We'll be here if you need us."

The strain flowed out of Branson's face, and he exhaled slowly. The nurse stepped quietly into the room behind Dane and Muriel.

BY THE MORNING, the doctors had decided Branson needed to stay for at least three days for observation. They said they would keep him on blood thinners and monitor his heart, help him manage the pain in his arm, and start him moving around as soon as he possible.

So Dane and Muriel went home alone.

For the first nineteen years of his life, Dane had lived in the same house. He had washed his clothes and eaten meals there sporadically for another eight or ten, and had visited irregularly ever since then. Never had the house seemed so empty to him. For the next three days, he and Muriel sat on the couch, worked separately, visited Branson at the hospital around lunchtime, and barely talked to each other. Sabine had no reason to come over if Branson wasn't there, so the brutal silence in the house went unbroken for hours at a time.

Dane passed the stairs to the attic a few times a day and looked upwards to see if he could detect any light coming from the window, any sound of voices, or anything that might give him a reason to go and take a look. He even crept inside and sat on the crate in front of the window a couple of times when he knew Muriel wouldn't find him there. But the attic remained as still and quiet as the rest of the place. Nothing interesting appeared through the window, just the neighbor on her daily run on the sidewalk or Muriel walking out to the mailbox.

And yet the house wasn't completely dead either, just silent. Dane would kiss Muriel before he got out of bed in the morning. Muriel would brush her hand across his chest when they passed each other in the hall or randomly rub his leg while they worked or ate side by side. A spirit of mourning filled the house, but the dearly beloved was still alive and supposedly making his recovery miles away in a room just a little more quiet and sterile than the house they lived in. They could have just gone to their condo to sleep and work and wait for the doctors to release Branson from the hospital, but still they stayed, because it felt like a holy communion, them keeping this vigil in this place. Something about the house was intrinsically connected to Branson. As long as they were there, they could feel his presence, sense his strength recovering, and know he would soon be home with them.

Besides, Dane spent much of the days listening intently to the things he didn't hear in the silence of his father's house. Obviously, he didn't hear his father shuffling around or talking to himself, turning on the television, or calling Sabine for something he needed. He didn't hear Sabine singing, mumbling some song in Creole as she prepared a meal or helped Branson around the place or got him ready for their walks.

For Dane, though, something else in the silence engrossed him, all the sounds he *didn't* hear were threatening to deafen him. He was acutely aware that he didn't hear any cartoons in the old house, any lullabies or sing-song toys. He didn't hear the thump and thud of feet running back and forth upstairs or jumping on beds. No doors slammed and no wails filled the air, the exhausted, inconsolable cries of a toddler so tired and overstimulated until he had lost the capacity for rational thought. Every moment he didn't hear those noises, he thought about asking Muriel if she didn't hear them too, and every time he started to ask, he backed off, afraid to hear her answer, and the silence continued for the whole three days.

On the third day, husband and wife sat on the couch, working side by side without talking, when the hospital called Dane's phone. He looked at

Muriel, who nodded for him to answer it. Still, he hesitated a moment longer. They both knew Branson should be discharged any day, but they still dreaded any news from the doctors. On the fifth ring, Dane put away his work and answered. The woman at the other end told him his father was ready to go home, and the doctor would be available to answer any questions he might have.

Dane thanked her and dropped the phone to his lap. He leaned forward, resting his face in his palms.

"Everything okay?" Muriel asked, her voice hitching with fear and a raspiness from not speaking for a couple of days. She dropped her laptop on the couch. "Is your father all right?"

Dane nodded and rested his hand on her thigh to reassure her. He looked into her eyes and smiled weakly, still nodding.

"I want a child," he said.

Muriel turned toward him but backed away just an inch or two on the couch. She looked into his eyes, studied them, as if she were unsure she had heard right, if there were any other way she could take this.

"I know it's too late," Dane went on, mashing the heel of his fist into his left eye socket without breaking eye contact. "I know we had a deal, and I'm changing it. I know that's not fair."

Muriel slid closer to him on the couch, put her arm around his neck and her forehead against his cheek. His face felt feverish and damp against her cool skin.

"I know you don't want to, and I know we're too old. I know I should have said something years ago." Dane took Muriel's hand with his left hand and placed his right hand on her hip, pulling her even closer. She pressed a kiss against his cheek and put her hand over his temple, holding his head against her lips.

"But this is all new. I don't know why," Dane said. "Maybe I'm just going through something. Maybe I'll feel different later. Maybe after Pop . . ."

Muriel pinched his ear hard and then stroked it gently.

"I don't think I will, though." Dane stroked back the curls of hair from Muriel's forehead and pushed her head away from his so he could see her eyes again. Her dark brown face shined with tears, beautiful in its softness. He thought if he looked close enough at her high cheeks, he might see himself reflected there.

"I felt like this was coming," Muriel whispered to him, "but I still don't know what to say."

"I don't know if it's losing Mom or taking care of Pop. I don't know if it's seeing you take care of him or just sharing the house," Dane said. "I'm sorry."

Muriel kissed him and shook her head. "You don't have to apologize for feeling this way," she said, "or any way."

"Haven't you felt it, too?" Dane asked. "The house so empty and quiet? Whatever spirit or magic in it just gone?" He swiped the back of his hand across his face and then took both of her hands into his lap. "What are we going to do? For the rest of our lives? When we're Mom and Pop's age? Who will I have when you're gone?"

Muriel held his face and passed her thumb over his lips. She smiled at him. "You really are determined to outlive me?"

Dane smiled a little and held her hand to his face.

"*Ké mwen*, I love you," she said, "I can see how much you want this."

She kissed him in the middle of his forehead, on each cheek, on his lips. Then she looked into his eyes. "I'm not having a baby. I don't want to be pregnant."

Dane nodded and rested his face in the hollow of her neck.

"But maybe," she whispered in his ear, "maybe there's a baby out there who needs us."

Dane jerked his head up so quickly that he almost caught Muriel's chin. He narrowed his eyes and looked at her, and she smiled back at him.

"I'm not saying yes," she said quickly, "but maybe there's a baby who needs a good home." Dane looked away, a confusing mixture of hope and disappointment running through him in waves. Muriel turned his face back towards hers. "And a good father."

Dane looked into her lap and said nothing.

"We can talk about it," she said. She kissed each of his eyes and Dane's face cooled, his tears stopped. "Let's go get Dad."

Dane nodded and said he needed to go upstairs to get his shoes on and wash up before leaving for the hospital. Once inside the bedroom, he sat on the edge of the bed, slumped forward, and tried to center himself. He felt as if he were falling, as if he were on a roller coaster with the feeling of weightlessness mixed with fear. He closed his eyes, pressed them hard. In the darkness, he saw the swirling lights from the pressure on his eyes, and the girl from his dreams stepped forward, smiled, and reached out for his hand.

WHEN THEY GOT to the hospital, Branson was waiting for them, dressed and sitting in a wheelchair. A blanket with pink and blue stripes covered his lap, tucked around his thighs, one of the same thin white blankets they used to wrap babies. The nurses said he had complained about being cold, so they brought it for him. It couldn't possibly have done much for the cold, but he stopped complaining anyway.

"Is Gwen here?"

Those were the first words Branson said when Dane and Muriel walked into the room. He looked so much better than he had just a couple of days ago. A healthy flush lit his cheeks, and his eyes widened with anticipation.

Muriel put her hand on Dane's chest, pushed him back so softly that only he knew it, and crouched next to Branson in the wheelchair. "Mom is gone, Dad."

Branson looked at her, confused. The flush drained from his face, and his shoulders fell.

"Gone?"

Muriel held his hand firmly and rubbed his forearm to the elbow and back. "She died two months ago. You sang at her funeral."

"She died." He had a puzzled look on his face, the same one he often wore now, but he didn't phrase it as a question.

Muriel kissed his cheek and patted his hand.

"Then nobody is at home?" Branson said, looking up at Dane and then over at Muriel. "Nobody's going to be at home with me?"

Dane rested his hand on his father's shoulder, felt the bone and gristle that used to be supple muscle. In that moment, he didn't see his coach or his tyrant, just a lonely and exhausted old man.

"We'll be there, Dad," Dane said softly. "We'll stay with you and sleep in the second bedroom."

A faint smile passed over Branson's face, and then it widened. The confused look passed from his face, and he reached up and placed his hand on Dane's chest.

"And Sabine?" Branson's smiled broadly with delighted recognition, like a little boy who's just conjured some happy memory.

Muriel clapped her hand to her mouth. She squeezed Branson's hand as hard as she dared and then backed off. Snatching Dane's hand from his side, she crushed it instead and held it tight.

"Sabine will be there, too," Dane said, "Sabine in the day, and me and Muriel at night, for as long as you need us."

Branson patted Dane's chest, and for a moment, they were a chain of energy and strength flowing through the connection around and around until the flush returned to Branson's face.

"I like that," he said.

A part of Dane fought against it, but his father's excitement about coming home proved too contagious to resist. The house had been so quiet and empty for the past few days, like a derelict ship with no one, not even ghosts, to steer it. Despite all the awkwardness between them, Dane looked forward to the bustle and the anxiety of having his father around again. He felt rejuvenated by the little break and encouraged by the way Muriel had responded to his thoughts about having a baby. Even some of the things Dane had found most annoying about living with his father and being responsible for him were now some of the things he eagerly planned for while they were on their way back home.

Dane wanted to push his father down the halls and out to the car, but the orderly insisted on doing it. Hospital policy. But as soon as the hospital valet pulled their car around, Branson seemed to leap out of the chair. The motion itself seemed sluggish, but it still hinted at the same agility Dane had seen the old man flaunt on basketball courts and dancing with his mother. Muriel eased him into the back seat and walked around to sit beside him, and Dane drove them home.

When they got home, Sabine was sitting in her car outside the house, reading something on her phone. She stepped out when they pulled up beside her and told them she had received the rehab plan from Branson's doctors. Branson went inside with her, and she got lunch ready for him.

The house came alive again. Branson moved slower and slept longer, but his infectious cheerfulness surged through the house, unaffected by the hospital stay or the health scare. Even within the first couple of days, he would have moments where he would forget all about the hospital. He would struggle against his sling and complain about the cast until someone reminded him of his broken arm, and that he would have to be careful with it for a few more weeks. But those moments passed quickly, and Branson seemed happier than ever.

Sabine shortened the walks and told Branson that his doctors wanted him to lift weights. She began taking him to the rehab center first twice a week and then three times. Every time they came back, she gave Dane and Muriel a glowing report of his workout.

"You should have seen him today," she said, stroking the old man's arm as well as his ego. "He was moving those dumbbells like some kind of beast, a football player or bodybuilder."

Branson smiled through his exhaustion. He flexed his arms and posed.

"Feel my legs, Dane" he dared, "feel the muscles."

It felt strange, but Dane obliged him, giving the old man's thigh a light pinch while Muriel giggled. The skin had grown looser and more wrinkled than Dane remembered seeing it, but sinewy muscle rippled under it, and he wasn't lying when he told his father he felt it.

The attic had started calling to Dane as soon as Branson came home again, creating a sense of urgency that pulsed through him every time he passed the stairway. Despite the harmony and optimism permeating the house, it took a few days before he found the courage to make his way up to the attic again. What he saw up there, the new things he would learn, could flood him with peace and bring him a step closer to his father, or just as easily reveal things he would rather not know. He had plenty of opportunities, with Branson sleeping more in the night and spending more time out of the house in the day, but every time he found himself at the base of those stairs, he wondered how much more he needed to see. He knew he had a greater love for his father now, but how well did he really want to know him? Was he better off not knowing everything about the people he loved? If he could see Muriel's secrets, all the hidden places where she had not granted him access, would it be worth the risk to take a look? If she could know everything about him, what would he hide?

But soon his curiosity overpowered all those fears and questions. Dane woke suddenly on the third night, with his arms still wrapped around Muriel and his left hand tingling from the circulation being cut off. He slipped his arm from underneath her and sat up, his After rubbing his arm from the shoulder down and turning his wrist around and around to get rid of the pins and needles, he stepped into his sneakers. He looked behind him to see if Muriel still slept. Satisfied, he slipped out of the bedroom and upstairs to the attic.

When he opened the door, there because warm light flowed filled the room and stung his eyes. He thought someone had left a lamp on up, but then he remembered that he had cleared out almost everything, lamps included. Once he closed the door behind him, he covered his face against the brilliance blazing through the window like a beacon. As he drew closer, his eyes hurt as though he were walking into the sunlight after sleeping all night in a dark cave. He checked his watch. It was still not quite two in the morning, but through the window, the front yard baked in noontime daylight.

Pulling a crate in front of the window, Dane sat and focused on a couple of figures in the grass down in the front yard, blinking away sunspots until he could see properly. He recognized himself immediately, right down to his favorite sky-blue Star Wars T-shirt. The little Dane down in the yard had to be about eight, smiling and running around on the lawn with a wild look, running hard to get away from someone.

The other figure, the one his younger self was trying to escape, was his father. Branson was the exact copy of Dane's grandfather. They shared the same athletic build, the same cropped, early-graying hair, the same athletic and graceful way of moving. Young Dane didn't stand a chance. He tried to fake a turn, slipped on the grass, and went down fast onto his back.

Before he could spring back up, young Branson leaped on little Dane, wrapping him in a bear hug and throwing his head back in a victorious shou like a WWF wrestler. Then, in one easy movement, Branson grabbed the boy by the thigh and the upper arm and hoisted him high over his head. The boy, suspended at least eight or nine feet over the ground, kicking and flailing, wore the expression of a kid on his first roller coaster, all smiles and screams. Branson stretched to his fullest height, shook the boy up and down a couple of times and then let him fall without actually letting go of him, catching him just before he hit the ground.

For his part, the boy pretended to writhe in pain, yet kept laughing.

Dane smiled through the window, the memory of all this horseplay flooding back to him as he watched. He remembered the musky smell of his father's sweat and cologne, and the dizziness of the fall, the strength in his father's arm, and the hardness of his muscle.

Dane watched the boy and the man roughhousing on the sunlit grass through the window, and he reminisced. The father had the boy pinned down, wiggling and struggling and giggling under his weight. With a dramatic flourish, the father acted as if he had been thrown off. He shook off his mock surprise, and donned the angry look of the wrestling villain. He drew up his arm and prepared for a mighty elbow drop just as the boy sprang to his feet for a fresh attack. The man's falling elbow crashed into the face of the boy jumping upward, and instantly, a gush of blood spurted from the boy's nose.

Dane winced and instinctively covered his own nose, feeling a pain produced by a mixture of memory and sympathy. He half expected to feel the blood flow underneath his own fingers.

The boy dropped to his knees on the grass and froze there, his eyes fixed on the blood smeared across his hand. The man standing over him also froze, his shoulders hunched over, making him look a few inches shorter. After a moment, the boy opened his mouth and screamed. In one motion, the man had his polo shirt off and wrapped around his hand. Kneeling in front of the bloody-nosed boy, he pressed his wrapped shirt into the boy's face, gently pushing his head back and down. With his other hand, he stroked his son's back, soothing him.

After a couple of minutes, the man slowly pulled away the shirt, now stained with a circle of blood. He moved his face close to the boy's, shifted the small head one way and then the other, inspecting for more blood flow. Then he gently pinched the bone at the top of the boy's nose between his thumb and forefinger, and they both laughed and went into the house.

Why had this moment slipped away from Dane? It wasn't such an important one, but certainly better than all the memories of leather belts, heavy hands, and harsh words. Somehow, this memory lived inside of Dane, yet it had not seen the sunlight of his thoughts for decades. He had dwelled on memories full of pain and anger, taken them out and turning them over and over countless times like a child plays with a favorite toy until he knows every edge and surface of it. But this one he had forgotten.

Dane looked through the window for at least an hour. Cars passed by in the street, but no one came back out of the house. Once Dane had watched the sunset through the window, he got up and quietly returned to his old bedroom, slipping into bed next to Muriel. Before he fell asleep, he tried to remember every time he and his father had happily played together in the front yard and the when the games ended.

BRANSON STARTED SLEEPING later and later in the mornings. Sabine advised him if he wasn't up and around when she got there, then she would have to get him moving. The doctors had been very clear. He should rest when he needed it, but sleeping too much didn't bode well for his health and would certainly slow his heart recovery. But the first Saturday after Branson's heart attack, it fell to Dane to get his father up in the morning, which meant he had to get himself up first.

Muriel had insisted that Dane sleep on the open side of the bed, had even set an alarm on his phone when he wasn't looking, knowing he would be reluctant to get started. For the few weeks they had lived in the old house before Branson's accident, getting up on Saturdays had never been a problem. The old man generally got up with the dawn and started patrolling the house. He would sit on the couch watching television or looking out the window until Dane dragged himself downstairs. Now, however, the doctors warned that he might sleep as late as they let him.

When the alarm went off at eight in the morning, a time Muriel and Dane had agreed was not only reasonable but generous, Dane didn't react. When it went off twice more, Muriel jabbed her elbow into his back. In the tiny bed, she could only manage a poke rather than a punch, but it got Dane's attention. He reached down for the phone on the floor and touched the screen to stop the cacophonic sound, and rolled over to face Muriel, draping his arm over her waist. She smiled and kissed him, then pushed against his hips until she forced him to either swing his feet to the floor or fall out of the bed.

Dane slipped into flip-flops and staggered out of the room, blowing a kiss over his shoulder. He crossed the hall to his father's room and found the door already open a couple of inches. Knocking lightly as he pushed the door in, Dane peeked through the gap and saw an empty bed, the covers tossed aside. He turned to check the bathroom before going downstairs to the kitchen, but he heard a whimpering, pained sound coming from the attic before he reached the bathroom door. Dane struggled to remember if he had locked the attic door. He hadn't bothered keeping it locked while Branson was in the hospital, and now he couldn't recall doing it since they had brought Branson home.

Suddenly fully awake, Dane bounded up the stairs, skipping two or three steps at a time. Reaching the top, he burst forward, throwing his shoulder into the door and falling to his knee on the other side.

Sitting on his crate in front of the window, he nearly fell as he twisted around to face Dane, as if startled out of a dream, his broken arm swinging against his chest in its sling. The old man's eyes were bloodshot and glassy.

"Are you hurt, Pop, I mean, Dad?" Dane said, pulling himself to his feet. "Do you need some pain meds?"

Branson just turned away, looked through the window, and whimpered again as if he were hurt. Dane walked up behind him and laid his hands on his father's shoulders, partly to comfort him but also to feel the muscles there and see if he could find the source of the pain. He looked down over his father's head through the window and saw a silver 1980 Toyota Corolla parked on the curb.

. As soon as he saw the car, he knew what would happen next. His hands tightened on his father's shoulders. Branson squirmed under him until Dane realized he was hurting the old man. He let go.

Through the window, Dane saw a thirteen-year-old boy step out of the car wearing a basketball uniform in the blue and white of his school colors. Dane knew the boy's age because it was him and because he remembered every detail of that day, one of the clearest memories he had of his father, and the one he revisited most frequently in his mind.

On the first day of the district championships for his junior high squad, Dane had played forward and his father had coached the team. The entire experience of playing with his father as a coach felt awkward even on the best days and thoroughly bitter on the worst. He spent every practice feeling as though he were pinned under a microscope. His father enlarged and distorted every one of his mistakes, creating a grotesque fun-house image of Dane. Dane endured every game with dizzying anxiety. Every shot he took carried the weight of a game-winning point, and his hands sweat and trembled every time he touched the ball.

The boy leaning against the car knew that every one of his teammates felt the same way about the coach, from the starters all the way to the water boys, but the boy was the only one who had to go home with him. For the rest of the team, the practice, the game, and the scrutiny ended at the doors of the gym. But the awkward, gangly boy with mismatched legs found no shelter from the scathing and oppressive eye of his father and coach. He couldn't bear to go inside and endure his mother's pity, but he couldn't stand one more second in the car with his father's criticism, so he stayed put, leaning against the silver car and fighting back the thing heaving his chest and burning his eyes.

They had lost so badly that the referees invoked the mercy rule, running the clock nonstop in the second half to mitigate the embarrassment for the losing team, so clearly outmatched. It killed the boy to know they could have played better. He knew they were a better team than those forty-five minutes proved. They had even beaten this team at the beginning of the season, but the pressures of success, the prospect of advancing in the region, and the coach's constant shouting from the sideline made them second guess themselves and fumble through the game until the scoreboard mocked their defeat.

The man stepped out of the driver's side and walked around to where the boy leaned against the hood, crossing defiant arms in front of his heaving chest. The man wore a furrowed and reddened expression signaling an explo-

sive mixture of anger and embarrassment. Without looking at the boy, the
man pulled him by the arm as he passed. The boy stood firm and resisted the
man's controlling hand. He jerked his arm out of the man's tight grip.

The man turned, this time looking his son in the face. In a flash, his hand
snapped forward, slapping the boy in the back of his head. The strike had
enough force to make the boy trip forward, off-balance, but he stayed on his
feet, if only by luck and will.

The man shouted something at the boy. Up in the attic, standing beside
his aged father, Dane couldn't hear a thing, but he still mouthed the words
anyway. *Stop crying, you sissy.*

The boy's hands dropped to his sides, curled into fists. He squared off
with his father and shouted back at him. In one motion, almost too fast to see,
the man ripped his belt from his gray slacks and held it tightly by the ends.
Before the boy could put his hands up defensively, the belt fell on him, curling
around and blistering his upper thighs. Again and again, the belt whipped
around him catching his hip, his leg, his lower back.

The man grabbed the boy by the arm, tried to yank him around so he
could get a better view of his backside, but then the boy did something he
hadn't done before.

Up in the attic, his hands still resting on Branson's shoulders, Dane held
his breath, remembering the feeling and the weight of that moment, how even
in the second before it happened, he felt the gravity of it, knowing something
essential had just broken in him, and it might never be repaired.

The boy wrenched himself free of his father's grip and grabbed the curled
end of the skinny black leather belt with his left hand as it swung a third time.
It smacked into his hand, and his fingers closed around it tightly. For a moment, father and son were tethered by pride and anger as much as by the cord,
bound to each other in a contest where neither dared let go.

The boy on the lawn would never let that belt go, never allow himself to
be hit with it again. As far as he was concerned, he was a man now, almost as
tall as his father and better than him too, in just about every way his childish
mind could imagine. Whatever this man had meant to him before faded from
his mind, buried under a pile of scolding insults and physical rebukes. The

man on the other end of the belt was an enemy, nothing else.

With his free right fist, the boy swung wide and landed a haymaker flush on his father's jaw. The man staggered back a step, let go of the belt, and brought his hand to his face. He seemed stuck for a moment, stunned either by the blow or by the audacity of the boy.

Dane felt Branson's shoulder and neck muscles tighten under his hands as if he had just taken the punch all over again. Branson drew in a deep breath and let it out in a stuttering exhale, shaking as he slumped on the crate, but he never looked away from the window.

The boy downstairs must have been equally stunned because he just stood there, holding his ground but not moving, not advancing. His fists were back by his side, his knuckles just reaching the bottom hem of his basketball shorts. His face burned with all the rage and defiance he could muster.

Then the man sprang forward and grabbed two fistfuls of the boy's jersey, the blue and white numbers twisting in his hands. He drove the boy back against the car hard enough for his head to snap backward and bounce off the Corolla's roof. Without losing the momentum of his charge, he let go with his right hand and smashed the boy's midsection with a powerful punch, right beneath the ribcage. The boy's mouth opened wide, and every bit of air emptied from his lungs. His knees buckled and gave out beneath him. As he fell, one hand held onto his father's arm and the other grabbed a fistful of his polo shirt, partly to hold himself up and partly stop the next blow.

The man pulled the boy to his feet and pressed him against the side of the car, shouting something Dane couldn't hear through the window, but he remembered every word. Before the man could attack again, the boy's mother ran across the lawn. She placed a firm hand on the man's shoulder and tried to force her body between the two men. Even from the height of the attic window, Dane could see fear and disgust and love in her face, anger mixed with compassion.

The father let go of his son, and the son let go of his father. Still unsteady on his feet, the boy let his mother support him up the steps and into the house, leaving the man heaving deep breaths, standing on the curb.

Dane remembered every second of that fight. The next day, he had quit the team and only tried out the next year because his father had quit coaching his team, choosing instead to lead a city travel team in a nearby neighborhood. After that day, his father never attended any of his games, even through high school and college.

The heat and hatred of that afternoon had turned to embers over time but never quite died.

Dane's eyes remained fixed on the man slumped on the curb while the boy went inside with his mother, cursing his father. Dane watched the man, the shadow of his father, and saw all the rage and venom drain out of him, until there was nothing left to hold him up. He crumpled into the grass, just as his son had done. On his knees in plain view, he lay in a heap between the street and the house, his head in his hands on the ground as if groveling in prayer.

Minutes passed, and the man on the grass made no effort to move or get to his feet. When he finally raised his head, his eyes blazed red and tears streaked his face, where the indentations of the boy's fingers still glowed. He pressed one hand against the car to steady himself, rose to his feet, and walked into the house with his chin in his chest.

Dane stared at the spot in his lawn, living several moments at once. In one moment, he remembered how the boy had gone to his bedroom reveling in the manly blow he had struck, counting all his justifications with kicks to the walls of his father's house. In another moment, he saw a very different angle, watching the effect the fight had inflicted upon his father, realizing how much a father might grieve his own mistakes, even if he can't admit them or even believe he can change. In yet another moment, he looked through Branson's eyes, and felt the man's fear of himself and the things prowling inside.

Dane felt Branson's shoulders heave and then disappear. When he looked down, Branson's face rested in his one good hand leaning against the window, his other arm dangling by his side in its sling. Lowering himself to one knee, Dane crouched down next to his father and stroked the hair back from his face.

Branson grasped Dane by the front of his shirt, pulled him in as if he were telling him a secret. Dane flinched and looked at his father's face, saw tears wetting both sides entirely, and felt his own face flushed with wetness too. He put an arm around his father and wiped the tears from his face.

"He was such a good boy, and I was such a bad father," Branson said.

Dane pulled his father close and held him tight. The clouds shifted outside, and sunlight streamed in. It made his face feel suddenly hot and flushed. The labored sound of the old man's breathing echoed in the empty space of the attic.

"Dad," Dane whispered at the side of his father's head, "I wasn't such a good kid." He wiped the wetness from his own face with his palm and then wiped his palm on his pajamas. "And you weren't a bad father. You did your best."

"I couldn't get close to him," Branson said, clutching now at the back of Dane's neck, "and I don't think he knows how much I love him."

Dane stroked his father's hair for a minute, the two of them forehead to forehead. The light through the window warmed them both as the morning grew older and the sun filled the entire room.

"He knows," Dane said.

Dane held his father close. After a few minutes, it felt like the spell had broken. Branson said he was hungry as if he had forgotten everything they had seen and said that morning. But Dane remembered, and he thought about it all day, staying by his father's side in case he got tired, or hungry, or sad.

THE NEXT DAY, Sunday, Branson came out of his room dressed for church before Dane and Muriel had even gotten out of bed. He roamed in and out of the downstairs rooms and up and down the stairs.

"Gwen," he shouted, over and over, his voice growing more and more frantic. "It's time for church."

Dane pulled on his sweats and sneakers and dashed out of the bedroom, with Muriel behind him. It took a minute to figure out where his father's voice was coming from, and it moved from room to room through the house faster than Dane would have expected.

The idea of Branson getting outside, especially in such a confused and agitated state, worried Dane. Peeking into his father's bedroom, he saw the television on, playing a church service broadcast. Before he knew it, he could hear his father's voice, yelling now, from directly above him in the attic.

"Where's Gwen?" he yelled. "Where's all her books? Where's my things?"

Muriel ran up the stairs to the attic door, moving past Dane on the landing, taking two steps at once. She reached for the doorknob. From behind the door, Dan heard Branson grunting now, as if under some strain, and suddenly the sound of wood crashing and splintering against wood. Dane caught up with Muriel at the door of the attic, but she hadn't opened it.

"There's something against the door," she said, pushing it. "I can't open it more than an inch."

Dane looked through the slender opening of the door and saw the bookcase, and then both bookcases piled up and leaning against the door at different angles. He gripped the doorknob and pressed against the door as hard as he could with his shoulder, but it only budged half an inch.

"Gwen!" Branson shouted from behind the door and through the fallen furniture, his voice breaking from the strain.

"Stay here and talk to him through the door," Dane said to Muriel. "See if you can calm him down. I'll be back in a second."

Dane ran downstairs, stumbling as he turned around at the landing. He snatched his phone from the nightstand in the bedroom and continued down and out the front door. Once he got onto the lawn, he dialed Sabine's number and set it on speaker, desperately hoping she would know what to do Through the window, he could see his father—at least the top two feet of him—thrashing around the room with his good arm and yelling.

As the phone continued to ring with no answer from Sabine, Dane waved his arms around wildly, trying to get his father's attention, to get him to focus on him and calm down. Upstairs, Branson threw a crate across the room, yelling something Dane couldn't make out.

Then Dane saw his father suddenly look through the window, all the anger and strain evaporating from his face. He stopped waving his arms and jumping. His boyish smile returned, as if nothing had happened, like a small child distracted from a great hurt by some new toy.

Dane hung up the phone and put it into the pocket of his sweatpants. He rested his hands on his knees and doubled over to catch his breath. When he straightened again, he saw Branson smiling hypnotically through the window. Dane waved at him, but the old man didn't seem to notice. Instead, he just sat by the window and stared down into the yard, grinning with his eyes as much as his mouth.

Muriel ran out through the front door. "What's happening?" she shouted, Dane's gaze up to the window. "He stopped making noise. Can you see anything? Did he fall down or something?"

Dane took her hand and squeezed it, pointing up at the window with the other hand. "He looks calm for now."

"Thank God."

They stood there holding hands, their heartbeats winding down and their breath slowing. Mesmerized, Dane watched his father sit there and smile and laugh at whatever he was seeing through the window's curved glass.

To Dane, the old man's face looked not only happy but hungry, as if he saw something he loved more than anything in the world, something that charmed and consumed him. He leaned into the window, pressed his hands into the curved glass, and rested his smiling face on the top of the frame.

Then he unlocked the window. It swung open, just an inch at first and then all the way.

Muriel sprinted through the front door while Dane jumped and screamed on the front lawn, waving his arms madly, desperate to catch his father's attention and break the spell that had come over him.

"No, Dad!" he yelled. "No, no, no. Close it, Dad!"

The old man looked down into the yard, but Dane knew Branson was looking through him, not at him. His face and shoulders relaxed, and his smile beamed with pure tranquility.

Branson leaned through the window, just his head, with one hand on the jamb and the other hanging in its sling. His elbow bounced against the edge of the window frame, but he didn't seem to notice. Dane stopped shouting and ran into the house and up both flights of stairs, straight to the attic door.

Muriel pressed her back against the door in a squatting position, her feet pushing against the floor hard enough to make her sweat. The door wouldn't move. Dane drove his shoulder against the door, right by the knob, and pushed with her. The door budged about an inch, and then another. The top hinge of the door loosened and came away from the jamb just a bit.

"Get back," Dane grunted at Muriel.

Immediately, she stepped back toward the stairs. Dane crouched even lower into a bear crawl and rammed the door below the knob with his left shoulder. Once, twice, three times, each time opening the door a couple of inches more. On the fourth pass, he felt a sharp pain tear through his shoulder and all the way through his chest, so he pivoted to his right and rammed his other shoulder into the door twice more until the gap opened six inches wide.

"Okay, stop," Muriel shouted, stepping over Dane as he slumped onto his hands and knees. She squeezed into the narrow space, turning her head and grimacing as she forced the rest of her body through.

By the time Dane got to his feet, cradling his left shoulder, he had heard one of the bookcases slide and drop.

"Try now," Muriel called through the door.

Dane pressed against the door with his hip and right hand. It still resisted him, then slowly gave up ground until he could squeeze through. He stepped into the attic, hot from the effort and the morning sun streaming in through the open window. Bolts of electricity shot through his shoulder with every heartbeat, and his chest burned from scraping through the narrow doorway. Muriel crouched beside Branson with one hand on his back and the other on his cheek.

The window yawned wide open, and Branson leaned against the opening, his good shoulder supporting his upper body, his head hanging so low, his chin pressed against his chest. Muriel lifted his face and held it in both of her hands, like a mother inspecting a hurt child. He smiled just as brightly and peacefully as Dane had seen him from below.

"I think he's gone," she said, and her voice hitched into a sigh.

"How can you tell?" Dane crouched next to her and stroked his father's hair away from his eyes while she held his hands. "Are you sure?"

Muriel shook her head, only breath coming out at first. With her eyes still locked into the old man's, she gestured with her head toward the window. "Look outside," she blurted out.

Dane turned and looked through the open window. Downstairs, in the driveway to the left, he saw his own car, just as he had left it. Across the street, a couple of the neighbors had come outside, and at least a dozen or so people stood in their yards, hands on their hips or shading their eyes from the bright sun, all looking up at Dane through the window. One older man crossed the street at a little trot and called up to Dane from the sidewalk, "You all okay up there? Need any help?"

Dane waved him off and closed the window. He watched for a moment as the man crossed back to his side of the street and stood there, one hand shading his eyes as he looked up at the window.

"Call Sabine," he said to Muriel.

She nodded, rested Branson's head gently into Dane's waiting hands, and walked out of the attic. Dane watched her as she left, how she stepped neatly over the bookcase as she passed through the doorway, how her shoulders shook and one hand covered her face while the other drew her phone out of her back pocket.

Once she slipped through the doorway, Dane carefully pulled his father off the crate and onto the floor, the old legs straight and spread out in front of him. He lowered himself to the floor too, with his back against the wall, and drew his father close until the old man rested against his chest, seated between his thighs.

He passed one arm underneath his father's shoulders and the other across his stomach and looked into his face. As he studied his father's impish smile, those playful eyes squinted in the corners, Dane let all the tension and tightness leave his own face until he only felt the heat of flowing tears.

He looked away for a heartbeat, looked up at the ceiling, through the window, and then forced himself to look back. Faintly, somewhere outside himself, he heard Muriel on the phone, but again, he shut out everything else and just studied his father's face.

He thought about all his memories of this man, how many he would have to revise or throw away, which ones he would keep, which ones he might not be able to keep when his time came. But this memory, this picture, this smile, he wanted to stick with him forever.

A SUMMER HAD passed, but to Dane, it felt as if he had been sitting in that church, in the front pew, just days ago. Again, Muriel sat next to him holding his hand, rhythmically rubbing the flesh between his thumb and forefinger, as if she could pass her strength to him through her touch. His other hand held a light green file folder with his notes inside. Even after all the things Dane had witnessed in the past couple of months, an uncanny sense of the past intruding into the present dizzied him. Two pivotal moments in his life blended together as he waited for his turn to tell all the gathered mourners what kind of person had left them for good.

However, this time Dane felt as if he had only recently come to know the person everyone had gathered to celebrate, a stranger he had met in May and barely gotten to know.

Dane leaned forward and peeked at Sabine, seated on the other side of Muriel. She stared straight ahead as if her gaze went over the coffin and through the back wall of the small church. Thinking about how much she had meant to his parents, himself, and Muriel, Dane struggled to picture her, probably within a week, caring for someone else's parents, investing herself in some other life that would inevitably end up here. He wondered if the next family knew how valuable she would be, how her presence would become so subtly crucial to their lives. He doubted they could even comprehend the stony path ahead of them, and how much easier Sabine would make it.

The organist played the same old hymns she had played for his mother's funeral, the same small choir of about a dozen men and women sang along, and the same friends read the same verses, but it all felt very different for Dane. This time, he buried his father, the last of his blood. As he thought about it, the hand holding his notes trembled, tapping his leg with the rigid edge of the folder. How had he come to this moment so quickly? And how much time had he lost or squandered? A wall of grudges erected over years—decades—of animosity and stubborn iciness had ended in a single summer of desperate attempts to smash through it. In the end, he had barely created a crack wide enough to peek at the man on the other side. More than anything, even more than the loss of his father, the utter waste of time gripped Dane's spirit like a vise.

According to the program, his turn at the pulpit was approaching. It would soon be his duty to say the right words to best express his relationship with his father, what kind of man he had been, and what kind of life he had lived. And what could Dane tell them?

With his mother, he had felt like he had known her completely. He understood his feelings for her with no ambiguity. Even then, he found himself completely unable to express those emotions to a group of people who also loved her. Those last summer months spent with his father were the most time he had spent with the old man in more than thirty years. He learned so much about him, but still struggled to find the words to capture it all.

He pressed the flat of his hand onto the folder in his lap and felt a small, hard lump inside. Slipping his fingers between the leaves, he found his mother's ring still taped to the card. He traced its edge in a ceaseless circle, a way of distracting himself from the impossible task of eulogizing his father. Then the older woman, a friend of his mother whom he remembered from the last time he had been in this church, stepped down from the platform and smiled encouragingly at him, signaling his turn to speak.

Dane squeezed Muriel's hand once more before rising. He fussed with the front of his suit jacket, hesitant to climb those steps to the podium. But once he assumed his place there and looked out at the people gathered, he froze, astonished by the sea of faces in the pews, the balconies, the vestibule. So many people had come to honor his father. The church had been packed for his mother's funeral, but, of course, since he believed his mother had achieved sainthood, he expected no less than hundreds of pilgrims. But it had never occurred to him that the father he felt so conflicted about could have generated a similar effect on so many people. The difference in this crowd was not the size but the variety. His mother's funeral had been full of her friends, and there were certainly a lot of them, but this group included people of all ages. There were men Dane recognized from the church, but also referees and coaches his father had worked with over the years. There were younger men, too. Some of them looked about the same age as Dane—probably athletes his father had coached—and some were ten or twenty years younger. He never would have guessed his father had so many admirers. His mother's impact on the world might have been more palpable, but his father's reached farther.

A sudden quiet fell over his spirit, surprising him as he looked out to the crowd. When he had spoken over his mother, it had seemed as if every one of the faces he saw demanded something of him. *Move me*, they seemed to say, *make sense of this for me*. The weight of so many relying on him to deliver some inexpressible truth had suffocated him. This time, however, he felt no pressure, saw no demands in the faces he saw.

He didn't know exactly what had changed, the crowd or himself, but it certainly didn't feel as though he were there for them. It felt as if they were there for *him* and for each other as well, not coming with their hands open, claiming some stake in his grief, but stretching out their hands in support, feeling his grief with him and with each other. They weren't pressing him down but rather leaning on each other, supporting each other as they looked into their sadness together.

"My father was a complicated man," he began. At first, he startled himself with the sound of his own voice, but then the words flowed with a mysterious, almost unconscious ease. "He was often angry. I think some of you who played for him probably felt his wrath at one point or another." A murmur and a few chuckles rippled through the church, and Dane let out a clipped laugh as well.

"I envy some of you. There were times when he spent a lot more time with you, spent a lot more energy on you than he did on me." The laughter stopped.

"But then maybe that wasn't all Dad's fault." The last word hitched in Dane's chest. His eyes felt hot, and he looked down at Muriel, hoping to find some anchor there to hold him to the podium, to root him in this moment, but the sight of her tears clenched his own throat. He felt the awkward silence growing, but didn't know how to fill it. Opening the folder in front of him, he ran his hand over the contents. The cool surface of the embossed cardstock calmed him and spurred him forward. His fingertips caressed Valentine's Day cards from many years ago, relics of his parents' marriage.

He opened the one on top, a smaller card with a dark red cover made of velvet. *Every year grows sweeter*, it said in his father's handwriting. He touched his mother's wedding ring. Again, he traced the circle with the tip of his finger, and the last of the pressure drained from his chest and stomach. Very carefully, he lifted the edge of the tape, holding the ring to the cardstock, trying to avoid tearing the old paper. Freeing it from the card, he slipped the ring onto the pinky finger of his left hand. Even on his smallest finger, it wouldn't slide all the way to the base but hovered there next to his own wedding band.

"Sometimes, I think," he paused, looking over the edge of the podium at the ring on his father's hand, "if we hadn't had my mother to hold us together, my father and I would probably have parted ways as soon as I was able to leave the house. Without her, I don't know what kind of relationship I would have had with him. We both loved her—everyone did, really—and her love for us gave us value somehow. Sometimes we tolerated each other because if Mom loved someone, they must have some goodness in them, even if she was the only one who could see it.

"But I'm starting to see some of the things she loved about him. Too late, I guess." Dane looked down at Branson's face, the serene but blank expression created by the funeral home, and wished he could see his boyish grin, or even his furious scowl, just one more time. "He was a tough man, my father, in some of the best ways, but also in some of the worst. He could be a fierce protector sometimes, like a lion defending his pride." Dane spread the cards across the podium, glancing at covers which spanned a lifetime, decades of distinctively different art styles. "Sometimes, he let his fierceness loose on the wrong people. Sometimes he lavished affection on the people who made it easy for him. Sometimes he ignored the people who made it hard."

Selecting one of the older Valentines, Dane held it up for the congregation, showing the cover as he would a visual aide in his classroom. "I don't know why I saved these cards. I've thrown away so many things from my parents' marriage over the summer, but I couldn't let go of these."

Laying the open card down on the podium, Dane read the note written inside. "You make life worth living," he read aloud. "My father wrote that to my mom for Valentine's Day, probably a hundred years ago. She would write him these long poetic messages, and he would write back . . ." Dane opened another card. ". . . My heart belongs to you." He laughed, and several people in the church laughed with him.

"His heart did belong to her, though." Dane said. "It really did, no doubt about that." Closing his eyes, Dane remembered the way his mother's touch had the power to still all the rage in his father's heart. The two rings on his left hand clicked together as Dane opened a third card and read it to himself. *Every year grows sweeter.* "Maybe this was the best he could do."

Dane closed all the cards and gathered them into the folder again. "I'm going to keep these," he said. "I don't know why exactly, but I want to keep them. I've thrown away so much of my mother's things, and every one of them hurt to give up. Now I'm going to have to throw away my father's things, and I don't think it's going to hurt as much to let some of his things go, but I'm keeping these cards."

He looked at the ring on his pinky finger with its clear diamond scintillating in an ornate setting of curled gold. That was his mother's love. Over the podium, Dane could see his father's ring still on the old man's ring finger, a simple gold band with scratches all around it. That was his father's love.

Dane turned the plain band on his own ring finger and raked his thumbnail over a scratch on the gold surface.

"That's the best I can do," he said. "I'm going to keep the things about him I liked—the things I loved—and I'll just throw away the rest. Let go of it. I get to choose. And when I'm gone, I hope my . . ." Dane looked down at Muriel. The tears were gone from her face, and she looked up at him with pride. "I hope people do the same thing for me."

Dane tapped the folder of Valentines on the top of the podium, thanked everyone, and stepped down from the platform. He stopped at the bottom, in front of the coffin where his father rested. The old man's knuckles were large and knotty with age, from years of tapping calculator keys and scratching numbers into ledger columns, from snapping a leather belt and twisting a boy's ear.

They had smoothed his face with make-up, folded his hands in peace. Dane stifled a giggle at the thought of what his father would say if he knew he was wearing foundation and blush. They had made him look so different, without the strict scowl of the spartan man he knew, but he closed his eyes and pictured the sweet smile and calm brow he had only ever seen in the last couple of months of his father's life.

Still, if he looked at his father's face closely enough and in just the right way, he could see the boy who had withstood the kind of anger and violence that crushed most people. He could see the boy who had stolen a kiss from a pretty girl under a streetlight, and had fought for her honor. Dane looked harder, and chose to see the face of a man who had rejoiced in the birth of one child and grieved the loss of another. Those qualities were there because it was the face of a man, not a hero or a monster.

Dane chose to hold on to those memories and love the man who had lived them.

Acknowledgements

A FEW YEARS ago, a colleague and I talked about our fathers having Alzheimer's disease. Both of us had contentious relationships with our dads, both of us with lots of unresolved emotions and apologies left unsaid or unheard. The disease ravages its victims, robbing them of their personalities and their dignity, but sometimes it gives a little as well.

My friend, much farther down that road than I, counseled me that the last memories of his father had been sweet ones. It gave me hope. It made me think of my sister and brother, both of whom have similar unresolved emotions, real grievances for which they will never receive any acknowledgement, much less an apology. It's hard—devastating—to know that the entire burden of reconciliation rests solely on your shoulders and that you'll have to do all the work of forgiveness without the reward of relationship. It's even harder knowing that the person you need to forgive has forgotten what they did to cause the hurt you carry, and one day might even forget who you are.

But sometimes, it's the only path to peace.

I'd like to thank my parents, on my own behalf, for doing the best they could with what they had, and pray for my children's forgiveness for all my own failures.

Thanks especially to my beautiful and long suffering wife for putting up with a husband who sits in a chair in the corner tapping away at a computer until stories pop out. Thanks to my children and grandchildren—the bigs and the littles—for inspiring me not only to write, but to be the best man I can be. I love you all.

Thanks to my editors, Adrienne Horn and Deborah Froese at Indigo River Publishing, for all their patience and love and honesty, and for making me a better writer.

Thanks to my students and colleagues, because at least some of this book got written when I looked like I was working on school-related matters.

Finally, thanks to all the doctors, researchers, and caretakers working with those suffering from Alzheimer's. One day we'll talk dolefully about the dark times before the cure.